Des Was The Only Thing On Her Mind, And She Couldn't Get Him Out.

All Kit's instincts were shouting at her that earlier this morning, with very little effort, her encounter with Des could have turned from anger to passion. And if it had...

So much had happened today that was bewildering. Someone had killed Cody, and the sheriff was looking at her as a suspect. Even stranger was the fact that Des, whom she had avoided for years, had declared himself her lawyer, her defender.

She could cope with the sheriff, but Des was a different matter. She could well understand why for years women had made fools of themselves over him. At seventeen, she would have made a complete fool out of herself if he hadn't stopped their kiss. She groaned at her thoughts.

And this *would* have been a perfect night to relax—except she couldn't get her mind off the murder. And Des...

Dear Reader,

Happy New Year from Silhouette Desire, where we offer you six passionate, powerful and provocative romances every month of the year! Here's what you can indulge yourself with this January....

Begin the new year with a seductive MAN OF THE MONTH, *Tall, Dark & Western* by Anne Marie Winston. A rancher seeking a marriage of convenience places a personals ad for a wife, only to fall—hard—for the single mom who responds!

Silhouette Desire proudly presents a sequel to the wildly successful in-line continuity series THE TEXAS CATTLEMAN'S CLUB. This exciting *new* series about alpha men on a mission is called TEXAS CATTLEMAN'S CLUB: LONE STAR JEWELS. Jennifer Greene's launch book, *Millionaire M.D.*, features a wealthy surgeon who helps out his childhood crush when she finds a baby on her doorstep—by marrying her!

Alexandra Sellers continues her exotic miniseries SONS OF THE DESERT with one more irresistible sheikh in *Sheikh's Woman*. THE BARONS OF TEXAS miniseries by Fayrene Preston returns with another feisty Baron heroine in *The Barons of Texas: Kit*. In Kathryn Jensen's *The Earl's Secret*, a British aristocrat romances a U.S. commoner while wrestling with a secret. And Shirley Rogers offers *A Cowboy, a Bride & a Wedding Vow*, in which a cowboy discovers his secret child.

So ring in the new year with lots of cheer and plenty of red-hot romance, by reading all six of these enticing love stories.

Enjoy!

Joan Marlow Golan

Joan Marlow Golan
Senior Editor, Silhouette Desire

Please address questions and book requests to:
Silhouette Reader Service
U.S.: 3010 Walden Ave., P.O. Box 1325, Buffalo, NY 14269
Canadian: P.O. Box 609, Fort Erie, Ont. L2A 5X3

The Barons of Texas: Kit

FAYRENE PRESTON

Silhouette

Desire

Published by Silhouette Books

America's Publisher of Contemporary Romance

SILHOUETTE BOOKS

ISBN 0-373-76342-5

THE BARONS OF TEXAS: KIT

Visit Silhouette at www.eHarlequin.com

Printed in U.S.A.

Books by Fayrene Preston

Silhouette Desire

*The Barons of Texas: Tess #1240
*The Barons of Texas: Jill #1288
*The Barons of Texas: Kit #1342

*The Barons of Texas

FAYRENE PRESTON

published her first book in 1981 and has been publishing steadily ever since. This is her third novel for Silhouette Books, and she is delighted to be on board. Fayrene lives in North Texas and is the mother of two grown sons. She claims her greatest achievement in life is turning out two wonderful human beings. She is also proud to announce the arrival of her first grandchild: a beautiful baby girl. Now she has even more to be thankful for.

Prologue

Des.

The name of her stepcousin broke the peace of the cold winter morning and eased its way into Kit Baron's consciousness.

She didn't even flinch. As much as she hated the fact, Des Baron was never far from her thoughts, especially when he was in residence at the ranch, as he was now.

Like an apparition that haunted, Des—his dark eyes, his enigmatic smile, his long, lean body— seemed to hover, waiting for an opportunity to infringe upon her thoughts. It was crazy, and she had no answer for it. She simply had learned to endure until he once again left the ranch and she was able to breathe more freely.

As she continued toward the saddle barn, the gravel crunched beneath her feet and she forced her thoughts elsewhere. The dawn was just beginning to break over the horizon. All over the ranch, activity had been going on for hours. There had been a freeze during the night, but the day would warm up with the sun, and in the meantime, she didn't mind the cold. It cleared her head.

She loved winter mornings on the Double B, but then, she couldn't think of a day or a season she didn't adore. She had been born on it, and despite the harsh way her father, Edward Baron, had raised her and her sisters there, she had fallen in love with the land at an early age. Tess and Jill had gone in other directions, eager to be gone from the place and make their fortunes elsewhere. But now that their father was dead and Kit had had time to put her own personal stamp on the ranch, it was more than her home, it was her life.

Its wildness and unpredictability suited her down deep in her bones. She identified with the land that remained untamed, despite man's best efforts. It was her own personal kingdom.

As she drew closer to the barn, her steps quickened.

The saddle barn was a constant in her life. As a child, it had served as a place to hide from her domineering father, a place to dream of a happier life.

But even there, Des had managed to imprint himself on her memories. One summer evening, when she had been seventeen, she had fled to the barn after her father had verbally torn her to shreds over something so inconsequential she couldn't even remember what it had been. But she did remember Des Baron.

Coming into the barn, he had heard her crying. Following the sound, he had found her up in the loft in the farmost corner. Without a word, he had gathered her into his arms. But soon the comforting strokes had turned more urgent, and murmurs had turned into kisses. Soon heat was coursing between them. If he hadn't finally torn away from her...

But he had. And that night she had learned that Des was a danger to her like no other. With incredible ease he could make her want him to the point that nothing else would be important, make her fall beneath his spell until he was her entire world.

She couldn't allow it to happen.

Living under the heavy thumb of her father had made her vow she would never again allow herself to be dominated by a man. Once in a lifetime was more than enough.

And so, in public and on the surface, she had competed in an idiotic contest with her sisters to win Des's agreement to marriage. She and her sisters had each wanted to marry him because of business reasons that had to do with their father's will and, ultimately, control of Baron International, the family business. Privately, though, she had remained extremely wary of Des.

Damn the man.

Why wouldn't he stay out of her mind?

Just inside, she flipped on the light and started down the wide hall between the stalls. Immediately the scent of the sweet hay and straw, and the commonplace smell of saddle soap, leather and horses, enveloped her. Since childhood, she had equated the smells with comfort, with home, with safety.

She could hear Dia already moving restlessly in his stall, kicking out and whinnying nervously. Something had upset him.

With a frown, she made a fast stop by the tack-and-feed room, snatched an apple from the refrigerator, grabbed his halter off a peg and hurried to him. His head came up, his neck stretched out of the stall, and he nickered a greeting.

"Mornin', Dia," she said softly, giving him the apple and reaching up to stroke his neck. "What's wrong, boy? Did one of the barn cats get in your stall and spook you? Or are you just overly anxious for our run this morning?"

She knew she was. Whenever Des was home, she remained constantly on edge. And he had come in last night.

She rubbed Dia behind the ears, trying to soothe him with her presence and their well-known routine.

A sorrel quarter horse stallion with a blond mane and tail, Dia had been named Diablo by his former owner, who had cautioned her against buying the "crazy devil." Early in his life, Dia had been put into bad hands that had left him traumatized, with a hatred of all men. His former owner had been about to put the horse down. When she had found him, she bought him immediately.

She had spent two-thirds of her life under the

thumb of her father, who had been a devil of a man. In comparison, Dia was a lamb, though no one else on the Double B thought so. But then, no one else understood him as she did. Some men had the ability to crush a person's soul. Dia's soul had been crushed. She had restored it.

She opened the stall door and walked in. Dia practically pranced in place with eagerness. "I know, my beauty," she murmured as she slipped the halter over his head.

He loved their early morning ride as much as she did. It was their one guaranteed hour together, when no one bothered them and they could be alone with each other, the wind and the land. But it was more than eagerness for their ride that had him going this morning. Something else was up.

She cast a critical eye around the stall, then went outside again for a shovel. Turning the straw over, she failed to see anything obviously wrong.

She walked Dia out into the hall and crosstied him in the aisle. He pawed the sand beneath his hooves, and the other horses, sensitive to his mood, moved and nickered restlessly.

"I've been waiting for you."

The gruff voice sent a chill down her spine. She whirled around as Cody Inman stepped out of an empty stall three doors down. Suddenly Dia's nervousness made sense. "What are you doing here?" If there was a choice, no one ever entered the barn before she took Dia out.

"Like I said, I've been waiting for you. We need to talk."

Cody was a compact, muscular guy with dark curly hair, somewhere in his late twenties. He had been working on the ranch for about eight months. A couple of times he had been in the group she had gone dancing with. But last night it had inadvertently worked out so that it had been just the two of them.

With Cody at her side, she had flown one of the ranch helicopters into the nearest town, where she had heard there would be a good band playing, and for a short while she had enjoyed herself. But he had ended up drinking too much and had come on to her. As a result, she had been forced to cut the evening short.

Now she studied him, irritated that he had intruded on her private time. From the rumpled look of him, he hadn't been to bed, and from his slurred words, he had been drinking ever since they had returned.

As head of the Double B and everything on it, she was in charge of what was basically a man's world. She sometimes walked a fine line between boss and woman, but she was in no position ever to forget who she was. And she never did.

She had two rules. She played only with those who knew she was playing, and she never allowed the situation to get serious. She had thought Cody understood her rules. She had thought she could use their night of dancing as a shield to protect her from dwelling on Des and speculating on the reason he was home. She had been wrong.

Yesterday morning she had received an unexpected

message from Des, saying he was flying in and wanted to see her. She had panicked and set about to make sure she was busy.

Trying to avoid Des was a knee-jerk reaction with her, one she should have outgrown years ago. Still, going out dancing was something she had done a hundred times before with a hundred different ranch hands.

But no more.

No more.

If nothing else, this situation with Cody had taught her it was not a wise thing to do.

"Back away, Cody. You're making Dia nervous."

"Everything makes that devil nervous."

"I don't know where you're supposed to be working this morning, but it's not here." Though there were always exceptions, generally speaking only the ranch's longtime, most trusted hands were allowed to work around the main homestead, which was comprised of the main two homes and their support buildings. "Go sober up, then get to work."

She strode to the tack room and returned with a bucket of grooming tools.

He caught her elbow. "No way, sweetheart. I'm taking the day off. Besides, I'm with the boss. No one is going to get too bent out of shape over it."

His grip hurt. "Cody, you're drunk. Go do as I say."

"Don't tell me what to do! I'm not some common ranch hand. You and I clicked last night, and I'm not going anywhere until we've settled a few things."

She jerked away and went to Dia. At her touch, he calmed, but his skin twitched and the white rims of his eyes showed. "There's *nothing* to settle. Last night was fun, until you began to drink too much, but it's not going to happen again."

"Last night was special, you know that. But then you gave me the brush off, and that's not right. There can be something really sweet between us if you'll just let it happen."

She gave a sound of exasperation. "Tell me something. Am I speaking a language other than English? *Pay attention. Nothing* is going to happen between us."

"Come on, baby. You're a wild one, but I've made up my mind—*I'm* going to be the one who tames you."

"Tame me? Are you for real?" She used both brushes on Dia's back in an effort to hurry his grooming.

"Look, Kit, all I want is to go out with you again. What's so bad about that? We can have some more good times, get to know each other better."

"Do yourself a favor, Cody. Get out of my sight—*now*.

Even though she had done her best to keep her tone level, Dia must have heard something in her voice. He reared, kicked his hind legs out, then returned to pawing. "It's okay, boy."

She was able to get Dia's blanket and pad on without incident, but when she returned from the tack room with the saddle, Cody intercepted her.

"Come on, honey," he said coaxingly, blocking her path and grasping her shoulders. "We were hot last night. *You* were hot."

At his touch, true anger flashed through her. "Get your hands off me or you're going to be very sorry."

She pushed against him, using the weight of the saddle to throw him off balance. He staggered backward but quickly recovered. She turned away, but then heard him give a yell of anger. Before she had time to respond, his weight hit her back and she fell forward onto the saddle, hitting the ground and knocking the air out of her.

Dia gave a scream of fury and reared, but there was nothing she could do about him now. She rolled off the saddle just as Cody came down on top of her.

"Get *off* me, you bastard."

"No way, Sugar. You're mine now."

His lips crushed down on hers with bruising force, and she tasted blood.

She forced herself to relax for a moment, until she felt him loosen his grip and shift his legs. Then she jerked her knee up into his groin. He gave a loud groan and fell off her.

She scrambled to her feet and wiped the blood from her lip. "Collect your pay and be off the ranch by noon. You're *fired.*"

Cody groaned again.

She quickly saddled Dia and led him out of the barn. By the time her weight settled into the saddle, Dia was moving forward. She reined him in, attempting to hold him to a walk. "Easy, boy. Let's warm up first."

She flipped her hair free of her jacket collar, and as they passed the next barn, she saw Tio, one of the ranch's longtime cowboys, and lifted her hand to him.

"Kit?" he called out. "What's wrong? You're lookin' like thunder this mornin'."

"Just a guy who can't take no for an answer."

"Well, now, that ain't right, no sir. You want me to handle him for you?"

"Don't bother. I took care of him."

Free of the outbuildings, she eased Dia into a lope, then gradually into an easy gallop. When she thought he had warmed up enough, she let him run flat out.

The whole unpleasant scene with Cody could be traced back to her reaction to the news that Des wanted to see her. How incredibly stupid of her.

Des.

Where was he?

What was he doing?

Why did he want to see her?

One

Careful of her split lip, Kit took a sip of the hot coffee, leaned back in her rocking chair, propped her booted feet atop the porch railing and scanned the lake. The breeze rippled across its surface as the sun lit the water silver.

She hadn't meant to ride as far as the lake this morning. Normally she let Dia run for only a quarter of a mile, then slowed him to a lope for perhaps another quarter of a mile, after which they would head back to the barn.

But this morning neither one of them had seemed to want to return home just yet. So she had given in to the need to lengthen her time away from the waiting ranch business and turned Dia in the direction of her small cabin, which sat atop a bluff, overlooking the Double B's largest lake. She was glad she had.

Truthfully, Dia *never* wanted their morning ride to end. As for her, she was still upset about Cody. She cast her mind back on the few times she had been with him. For the life of her, she couldn't think of a thing she had done to lead him on.

But… Cody was a relatively new hire and didn't know her well. And they had been alone….

She sighed. In retrospect, it had been a mistake to invite him to go with her, but it was over now. Hindsight was a wonderful thing and, in this case, totally useless.

She took another sip and refocused on her surroundings. The lake cabin was one of her favorite places. As soon as her father had died, she'd had it built, along with a corral and a small barn. It had been one of her dreams. Here there were no phones. Here no one ever bothered her. Often she and Dia would ride out on a summer evening. She would swim and spend the night, then, the next morning, after another swim, she would head back to the house.

She scanned the lake. Unfortunately, it would be much too cold to swim this morning, and it was time she returned to her work.

A faint roar disturbed her musings. Curious, she got up and walked to the corner of the long porch so that she could peer around the side of the cabin. The roar was coming from the south, which meant it was coming from the direction of the homestead.

She shielded her eyes and picked out a vehicle,

speeding toward her at what she estimated to be well over fifty miles an hour, raising a cloud of dust behind it.

She stiffened. Surely it wasn't Cody. Surely their encounter in the barn had been enough to discourage him. But no...

It was a truck, she realized, as it drew closer. And it looked like the one her Uncle William had given his stepson, Desmond Baron, when he had graduated from law school.

Her pulse quickened, and her brow crinkled.

If it was Des, why would he seek her out here? His message had said he had wanted to talk to her. Was it so important he had felt the need to come after her?

It had to be him. No man on the Double B would dare abuse a ranch vehicle by driving it that fast over what was little more than a track. But with her Uncle William's death four months ago, Desmond Baron now owned fifty percent of the entire Baron empire. He could do anything he wanted to.

With a sigh, she sat her coffee cup on the railing and went down the steps to meet him.

If Des had been raised in a city instead of on a working ranch, his appearance might have stopped at classically good-looking. But he had been raised on a vast ranch and had conquered most of its jobs by the time he was fourteen. With time, the rough, out-door life had branded him with a ruggedness and sexuality that seared as hot as the West Texas sun. His thick, dark brown hair was styled away from his brow and in short sideburns in front of his ears. His brown eyes were as sharp and all-seeing as a hawk's.

With the force of his intelligence and personality, he had the ability to dominate any situation, whether it was in the courtroom, where he had earned a reputation as one of the toughest, smartest defense lawyers in the country, or on the ranch, where every hand viewed him with respect. He was as hard as the plains on which they had both been reared, so what did he want with her?

As he climbed out of his car, her heart somersaulted. She hadn't seen Des since the reading of the will, which had occurred right after Uncle William's funeral. Now his jeans wrapped his lean hips and long legs like a Christmas present. His boots were well worn, and beneath a sheepskin vest was a beautiful pine-green sweater. It looked hand-knitted, and she couldn't help but wonder if a woman had made it for him. The home where he'd been raised sat less than a mile from hers, and she'd had countless opportunities to watch him from afar, starting when she first became aware of him as a little girl. There had always been women in his life. Gorgeous women who seemed willing to do anything for him. She'd never liked any of them, not that it mattered.

His scent of leather and spice came to her on the breeze as he stopped in front of her. Funny. From the first time she had been this close to him, though she had tried her best, she had never forgotten the way he smelled. Or anything else about him, for that matter. "Good morning, Kit."

"Good morning." His sharp brown eyes seemed to cut to her very heart, and his deep voice resonated inside her. No wonder he won the majority of his cases. Just last week she had read that his latest trial had ended with a victory for his client. Most of the trials he conducted ended the same way. Opposing lawyers rarely had a prayer against him. "What are you doing out here?"

He paused, his gaze touching on her red hair.

"You really should have a phone installed out here."

It didn't escape her that he hadn't answered her question. "Usually I'm not here that long."

"Still, in case of an emergency, you should carry a cell phone."

His tone was mild, not dictatorial or judgmental. Nevertheless, she instinctively defended herself. "It's not like I'm out here all the time." She swung an arm to indicate her surroundings, causing her jacket to shift partially open and reveal her sweater. His gaze dropped to her breasts, and she silently cursed as she felt her nipples harden. "Besides, the ranch isn't going to fall apart if I'm gone for a few hours now and then."

"Actually, I wasn't thinking of the ranch. I was thinking about you. What would happen if you had an accident and needed help?"

She slipped her hands into the fleece-lined pockets of her jacket. "My managers know where the cabin is, along with my routine. If I was missing for more than a few hours, they'd come straight here."

"What happened to your lip?" he asked, causing her to take a quick mental left turn.

Her hand flew to her mouth and the split lip that remained slightly swollen. "I must have bitten it."

"Must have?" His gaze roamed her face, searching. "Don't you know for sure?"

"I bit it." She didn't want to tell him the truth. Despite her reassurances to herself, she still couldn't help feeling that she could have handled Cody better.

"It must have been a hard bite." He reached out and gently touched the spot. "And it looks like a fresh wound."

Heat flashed through her. She recognized the feeling from that long ago summer night when he had taken her in his arms. Why couldn't she forget? She moved her head slightly, dislodging his touch. "It's fine."

In a casual move, he shifted the lapel of her jacket aside, baring the portion of her sweater he had seen when she had gestured. "Is this your blood?"

She glanced down at her sweater. She hadn't realized her lip had bled so badly. That damn Cody. "What's brought you all the way out here? If you had just waited, I would have been back soon."

With a quickness that nearly took her breath away, he stepped forward and slid one hand along the side of her jaw, tilting her face up. "Kit, would you tell me if you were in trouble?"

His move and question took her by surprise. His touch warmed her skin. "I'm not sure what you're talking about."

"*Are* you in trouble? Because if you are, I'll help."

With his hand on her, she could barely think. Could he have heard about her argument with Cody? But no, that didn't make sense. For better or worse, she had taken care of the matter. "Why are you here, Des?"

He let his hand drop away. "You're needed back at the homestead."

"Why? I don't have any appointments scheduled until this afternoon." She didn't have a clue what he was thinking, and instinct honed over time kept her from trying to find out. With Des, it was better if she kept her distance. "Oh, never mind. I was about to head back anyway. I'll just close up."

"Wait."

His grim tone halted her as she was about to turn. She eyed him cautiously. Because of her father's cruelty in keeping her and her sisters under his thumb, and later, because of her wariness of Des, she'd never been close to him. But even she knew he wasn't acting normally. "What is it?"

"Someone's been killed, Kit."

"Oh no! Who?"

Death on the ranch wasn't a complete shock. Working with large animals, as well as heavy machinery and equipment, offered too many chances for accidents. But she always hated to hear about it.

"Cody Inman."

She stiffened. How could that be? After she had left, he hadn't even been supposed to go to work, only draw his check from the paymaster and leave. "Cody

Inman?'' she repeated to make sure she'd heard correctly. ''But I saw him right before I rode out this morning.''

''That's what Tio said. A little while after you left, Tio went into the barn to start his work and found the body in one of the empty stalls. Since you weren't around, he came to me. I called the sheriff, then drove out here to get you.''

She nodded. ''Of course.'' How had Cody managed to get into an accident on what should have been his last few hours on the Double B?

''How awful.'' However Cody had acted toward her, she felt a deep pang of sadness for him. Just last night he had been so alive, dancing and laughing with her. But then he'd begun to drink and come on to her, and then this morning...

Questions raced through her mind as she tried to grapple with the fact that a man she had argued with mere hours before was now dead.

''How did he die?''

''You don't know?''

Confused, she stared up at him. ''How would I know?'' He didn't answer. ''Des? How did he die?''

''It looks like a blow to the head with a blunt object. Perhaps a shovel.''

The air went out of her. ''Are you saying Cody was *murdered?*''

''That's right.''

''But I don't understand. How could such a thing have happened?''

"That's what the sheriff wants to question you about."

"Okay, I'll close up here and be there as soon as possible."

"No. Just leave Dia here and come with me. We'll have someone bring a horse trailer out for him."

"Is that really necessary?"

"The sheriff will be waiting to talk to you." He paused. "So, *now* do you want to tell me how you got that split lip?"

She hadn't told him. And for the most part, Des didn't say much on the drive back to the homestead, which was fine with her. She'd given him the general outline of what had happened, but no details. Her morning encounter with Cody was still not something of which she was proud. It had been a situation she had let get out of her control.

Thoughts of Cody and the way he had died kept her busy. She kept trying to come up with scenarios for what could possibly have happened, but for the life of her, she couldn't come up with one that made sense.

But then, Des also occupied a large part of her mind. She attempted to ignore him by fixing her gaze on the passing landscape, but time and again his nearness drew her thoughts and senses back to him. Despite her attempts to ignore him, it had always been like that. With resignation, she wondered if it always would.

When he finally pulled up to the saddle barn, she breathed a soft sigh of relief.

She didn't recognize several of the cars and trucks parked there, but she did recognize the sheriff from a picture she had seen in the paper, put there when he had first come to their area nine months earlier. A tall, lanky man in his late thirties, he stood beside one of the trucks, speaking on a cell phone, but as soon as he saw them, he hung up and waited expectantly.

"Have you had any dealings with this sheriff?" Des asked quietly as he cut off the engine.

"No. Any problems we have with the men we try to handle ourselves." Her hand went to the door handle.

"Wait a minute." Des leaned over and clasped her wrist, and his arm pressed against the softness of her breasts.

Heat filled her lungs and, uncontrolled, her nipples hardened. No matter what, she couldn't seem to stop herself from responding to him.

"Listen to me, Kit. The sheriff's name is Moreno, and his reputation is that he's ambitious. So I want you to say as little as possible, and when in doubt, let me answer for you."

"What are you talking about?" She pushed against his arm.

He straightened away, but the severity of his tone didn't lessen. "Don't volunteer anything he doesn't ask. And if I tell you not to answer a certain question, don't."

She glanced through the windshield at the sheriff,

whose gaze was now trained on her. "He just wants me to tell him what happened."

"Actually, he wants you to make his job easy by confessing. Right now, you're the only suspect for Cody Inman's murder."

Her mouth dropped. "Suspect? Confess? But that's ridiculous."

"It's also the truth. So just be careful what you say."

"This is absurd." Suddenly she felt as if she were suffocating. Cody was dead, and Des was focusing his entire attention on her. It was too much. Her legs were shaking as she climbed out of the truck.

"Ms. Baron." The sheriff touched the brim of his hat in greeting.

"Sheriff Moreno." Her nerves were strung tight, but there was no point in taking her mood out on him. It wasn't his fault. "Sorry to have kept you waiting, but I didn't realize anything was wrong until Mr. Baron came to get me."

Des stepped up beside her, and the sheriff's gaze shifted to him, then back to her again. She wouldn't have been surprised to see a hint of intimidation enter his expression. After all, Des had an international reputation as a lawyer, and she ran one third of Baron International, specifically the massive ranching division. But the man's demeanor remained businesslike and aggressive.

"I'll get right to the point. I understand you were the last person to see Cody Inman alive."

"No. The person who murdered him was the last person to see him alive."

"Of course."

Des was standing so close to her that the warmth from his body filtered through her clothes to her skin. She supposed it was his way of supporting her, but she didn't need his support, and she certainly didn't want it—at least, not this kind.

The sheriff once again glanced at Des, then back at her. "Let me put it this way. It looks as if you were the last person to see Cody Inman before he was murdered. In fact, one of your hands—"

"That would be Tio."

He checked his notes and nodded. "Tio Rodriguez. He indicated that you and Mr. Inman had had a problem this morning."

She nodded. "In fact, I fired Cody right before I left for my morning ride." Beside her, she felt Des stiffen.

The sheriff's brows shot up so high they almost disappeared beneath his hat. "You fired him? Was that because of something work related?"

Slowly, as if it were a perfectly natural gesture, Des reached out, circled her wrist with his long fingers and lightly squeezed. She felt something lurch near her heart. The questioning didn't bother her. Des, however, did. "No," she said, impatient to get away from both men. "It was personal."

"How so?"

"You don't need to answer that, Kit."

Des's sharp tone tightened her nerves, making her

response even quicker. "We went out last night and—"

"You and Mr. Inman? Just the two of you?"

"That's right."

"And what happened?"

"To put it as simply as possible, Sheriff, Cody wanted our relationship to go farther than I did."

"Kit—"

"And did you and Mr. Inman fight over this?"

"Kit! *Stop answering.*"

She glanced at him again. His jaw had tensed, and his eyes had darkened. "I've got nothing to hide. Cody and I definitely fought. But did I kill him? No, I did not."

"I see."

The sheriff didn't believe her, she realized with a small shock. On the Double B her word was law, and she wasn't accustomed to being doubted. Slightly shaken, she scanned the faces of the men who had gathered around him. Several of them looked confused, even skeptical. Great. Just great.

The sheriff nodded toward her lip. "Did you get that injury in the fight?"

"He kissed me."

"And the kiss split the lip?"

"That's right. He wasn't exactly gentle."

"Uh-huh. Made you mad, did he?"

"He made me very mad."

"That's enough." The authority in Des's voice cut between the sheriff and her. "If you need any further information, Sheriff, make an appointment with Ms.

Baron *through me*. Kit, I'll see you back to your house.'' His strong hand on her back quickly turned her and headed her back to the car.

"Wait a minute!" the Sheriff yelled. "Ms. Baron, I'll need to ask you to come down to the office. We'll need your fingerprints, and I'll want to question you further."

"She'll come in later," Des said, raising his voice, but not stopping until he had her in the truck and they were driving away.

Two

Kit slammed the front door shut in Des's face.

Damn the woman. A muscle clenched in Des's jaw as he opened the door and went in after her. He found her in the living room, lighting a fire.

"What were you thinking about, talking to the sheriff like that?"

She wheeled on him. Her green eyes flashed, vivid with anger, and her long red hair curled like flames against her shoulders. "Don't *ever* do that again to me."

"Do what? Save you from incriminating yourself?"

"Don't ever again tell me what to say or not to say. And don't *ever* give me an order in front of my men. You may own fifty percent of this ranch, but *I* run it.''

''Listen to me, Kit. You can't tell the sheriff everything you did without expecting to be arrested. Not in this case. Why didn't you do as I *said?*''

The logs began to burn behind her but she barely noticed. ''Do as you said?''

All of his career, he had faced hostile clients, lawyers, judges and juries. Part of his success was that he was always able to remain cool under fire. Staying calm and above the fray was one of his trademarks. No one ever got to him.

Kit got to him.

He wanted to shake her. Worse, he suddenly realized, he wanted to kiss her. Lord help him, where had that come from?

''Whether you realize it or not, Kit, you've gotten yourself into a serious situation. And just because it was *me* who gave you the advice, doesn't mean you had to go against it.''

''That's not what happened.'' She stripped off her coat and threw it across a chair.

''That's exactly what you did. Admit it. You hate for anyone to try to tell you what to do, but this case is different, and you need to realize it. In this case, you don't know what's best. *I* do. And believe me when I say, you told him entirely too much.''

She threw up her hands. ''For heaven's sake, get over yourself. The women you go out with must not have any brains, but I do.''

''You're not hearing what I'm saying. Dealing with

men like that sheriff is what I do for a living, and I know what I'm talking about. Let me do my damn job.''

"This isn't a job you need to concern yourself with. Whatever happened, happened in my realm. I'll take care of it.''

He shook his head. "Trying to defend yourself is the worst thing you can do.''

"I'm not trying to *defend* myself.''

"Then tell me what you think you're doing.''

"Telling the truth about what actually happened.''

He gave a sound of disgust. "Prisons are filled with people who told the truth. At this stage of the game, everything you say is important. Even *how* you say it. You have to be careful, and you weren't.''

"What are you talking about? The sheriff didn't indicate he suspected me.''

"If you believe that, you weren't listening.''

"Don't be ridiculous. Cody's body was just found. It's way too early for the sheriff to *suspect* anyone.''

"Granted, it's early, but have you ever heard of quick arrests?''

"Of course, but—''

"Ideally, authorities like to make an arrest within the first twenty-four hours of a crime. After that, witnesses can go foggy, crime scenes can be tampered with, or any number of other things can happen. Kit, face it. That's exactly what may happen here, because, unfortunately, it looks as if everything so far points to you.''

"That's not true. They haven't even found the murder weapon yet."

"Are you telling me that if the murder weapon turns out to be a shovel, or any one of the implements used in that barn, your fingerprints won't be on it?"

"No. They probably will be—" Abruptly she broke off and swiveled back to the fire. "I don't have my own silver-plated shovel, Des. At one time or another, I've probably used and touched everything in that barn."

She was electric, all fire and fury. But he also saw the fragility there. He had always been able to. He had often heard his adoptive father, William Baron, grumble about the stricter than strict way his brother Edward was raising his three daughters. He hadn't seen Kit on a daily basis or even a monthly one, but rather over time and at various stages of her life.

Living on the same ranch, he'd had a unique perspective from which to watch her grow up. As a little girl, she had tried in vain to battle against the tyranny of her father. As a teenager, she had become subdued and resigned to living beneath her father's thumb.

Her father's death when she was twenty had finally given her the freedom to come into her own, but that had also been when her rebellion kicked in. It had seemed to him that during those years she had been all flash and fury, yet she had also taken the reins of the ranch. Now she had everything she ever wanted, including power. The problem was, she now seemed to be rebelling against him. Worse, he felt the effects much more than he should.

He took a steadying breath, but it didn't have the desired effect. He couldn't seem to hold on to his objectivity. Deep down, he was frightened for her. Even more frightening to him, he was coming to realize he badly needed to keep her safe. Where had that come from? And when? "I'll put an investigator on this Cody Inman and find out about him."

"Don't be stupid. You won't find anything unusual about him. He was just an ordinary ranch hand."

"He was a man who hurt his boss, a woman. He tried to force himself on you, or have you forgotten?"

"Of course not."

"Odds are good that somewhere he's got a bad history, and I need to find out what it is. It could make a difference in the trial."

"Trial?" she practically sputtered. Her hair flew out around her as she spun around. "There's not going to be a trial—at least, not with me as a defendant."

"Calm down. I'm just thinking ahead. It's what I do."

Her brow furrowed with anger. "Who asked you?"

"Damn it, Kit—" He stopped himself and forced another deep breath through his lungs. He wasn't going to be able to help her unless he could regain his composure. Unfortunately, his temperature was rising by the minute.

She affected him way too deeply.

For most of his life he had deliberately stayed away from her and her sisters. Their father's will had stipulated that unless Kit and each of her sisters made his idea of a fortune within ten years of his death, they would lose their thirty-three and one-third percent portion of Baron International. Even though she was the youngest, Kit had already met the first condition of the will, earning that fortune plus more. Her sisters Tess and Jill had, too.

In addition, they had all known that his step-father, their father's brother, would leave his fifty percent of the corporation to him upon his death, which would essentially give him control of the company, unless the three of them voted together at all times, leading to a stalemate.

The sisters had quickly come up with the theory that if one of them could obtain control of his fifty percent of the Baron empire through marriage, she could thus control Baron International. So, like her sisters, Kit became caught up in the mad game of trying to get him to succumb to her charms. She and her sisters had actually competed to get him to the altar.

Most men would have reveled in the attentions of three beautiful women, but under the circumstances, he had decided reticence was the intelligent response. Fortunately for all concerned, the game had come to an abrupt halt when Tess and then Jill had married. In effect, they had given up everything for love and left the path to him wide open for Kit.

But then, suddenly, she had started to shun him. It didn't make any sense to him, and anything that didn't make sense bothered him.

She had always intrigued him, and now that he was

no longer preoccupied with his father's health or a trial, he had vowed that this was the trip home when he would find out why she was going out of her way to avoid him.

But now, just when he had decided to seek her out, fate had stepped in before him. A murder had put her in peril, and he wanted, needed, to help.

But she continued to confuse him.

She made his mind veer away from the subject at hand and on to the fact that she was the most desirable woman he had ever seen. At the moment she was practically vibrating with anger at him, yet all he could think about was how much he would love to kiss her.

The knowledge was a shock to his system.

He shrugged out of his vest and carefully placed it on the back of a sofa. "Let's go at this a different way. You told the sheriff that Cody had wanted to take your relationship farther than you did. What exactly was he to you?"

"Just a guy to go dancing with." She wrapped her arms around herself and began to pace. "I never meant it to be serious."

"Then why did you go out with him in the first place?"

She fixed him with a straight gaze. "Do you plan to take every woman you go out with to the altar. Or even to bed?"

"I've never dated a woman who ended up dead the next morning."

"Then obviously you've been lucky and I was unlucky. But believe it or not, I didn't know Cody was going to be murdered.''

He shook his head, frustrated beyond belief with her, with himself. And he knew what the problem was. He was letting himself get too involved, something he never allowed with clients. Yet even armed with that knowledge, he couldn't stop himself. ''Your flirtations have always been within inches of getting out of hand and you know it. It's called playing with fire, and sooner or later it was bound to get you into trouble.''

She made a sound of anger. ''You know *nothing* about how I handle my personal life.''

''I know enough. I've seen you on the dance floor with one guy after another, and, honey, let me tell you something. The way you dance is an invitation to every red-blooded male in the state.''

''That's *not* true.''

She looked as if he had struck her, but at least she was finally listening. ''It's true all right,'' he said, his tone grim. ''The last time I saw you at a party, you were wearing a little nothing of a white dress, and every man in the place was salivating.''

She stared at him, her green eyes wide and gorgeous. ''You remember what I was wearing?''

He frowned, as surprised at himself as she was. ''It doesn't matter. Let's get back to Cody. What happened when you were out with him last night that made him think he could have a future with you?''

Years ago, he'd had firsthand experience of how easily she could melt against a man. Even now, just looking at her made him want to grab her into his arms and make love to her. In fact, he couldn't get the idea out of his mind. So he didn't even want to think of her in another man's arms. The very idea infuriated him.

She made a vague gesture. "Nothing extraordinary happened."

Nothing extraordinary. She would probably classify the kiss they had shared in the barn all those years ago as nothing extraordinary, too. Hell, she probably didn't even remember it. But he did. He always would.

He crossed to her and gripped her arm. "That's where your faulty thinking comes in. *You* are extraordinary. You turn those green eyes on a man, you press that sweet body of yours against him, and I guarantee a man's going to feel something."

He couldn't help himself. He pulled her against him, and his throat went tight. He hadn't felt her body against his since she was seventeen. Then he had kissed her and hadn't wanted to stop. Now he felt the same way. It was completely inappropriate. It was totally astounding. "Exactly *how* hot and heavy did you get with him?"

She twisted, trying to free herself. Her breasts and thighs rubbed against him, making him hard. What little control he had left was about to disappear. Suddenly he was quite sure he was about to do something irrational, and abruptly he let her go. He needed to help her situation, he reminded himself, not harm it. He needed to remain clearheaded.

Looking shaken, she rubbed herself where he had gripped her and moved away. "Hot and heavy? Charming phrasing, Des. Really charming."

It was a clumsy phrase, but his vaunted word power had deserted him. He drove stiffened fingers through his hair. He knew better than anyone the need to keep personal feelings out of this, but the thought of her in danger made him crazy. "You know what I mean."

"*No.* In no way did I lead him on. *Furthermore,* nothing hot and heavy happened. At the bar, he forced a kiss on me and I brought the evening to a quick halt."

"And after that, what happened? Did he just accept your decision?"

She shrugged. "He got a bit sulky. After we got back to the ranch and I went to drop him at the bunkhouse, he tried to kiss me again, but he didn't get very far."

"How did you manage that?"

"I had one of the guys at the hangar secure the helicopter for me, I dropped Cody off, then I came home."

"And do you know what he did after you left?"

"I don't have a clue. Except…"

"Except what?"

"Well, it was obvious this morning that, whatever else he did, he went off and began drinking heavily. When we were together, he had two beers."

"How many did you have?"

Resentment flared in her eyes. "None of your business."

"Someone's going to ask, Kit. It might as well be me."

"I had one. Okay? I had one."

"Is that usual for you?"

"What are you getting at?"

"To your knowledge, has anyone where you were last night ever seen you drink a lot? Or even get drunk?"

"No." Her eyes darkened with her anger. "Do you honestly believe I would have had more than one beer when I was *flying* home?"

He studied her for a moment, believing her and wondering how his planned quiet talk with her had turned into this angry confrontation. Then he silently answered himself. He had just realized that he cared too much. "Okay. You said you dropped Cody at the bunkhouse. Did anyone see you drive off in your car alone?"

"Probably. What difference does it make? I was dropping him off at the bunkhouse."

"When you're involved in a murder case, you have to backtrack and look at every single detail. For instance, the person who saw you two drive away from the hangar together could have thought that you were bringing him here. He could have assumed you two were lovers, and if the sheriff heard that, he could have decided you two had a lovers' quarrel and you killed him in a fit of rage. It happens a lot."

"But it *didn't* happen in this case."

"Had you slept with him, Kit?"

"*No.*"

The relief he felt was out of all proportion to what it should have been. "When you're involved in a murder case," he said quietly, "you have to look at everything."

"But *I'm* not involved." She started to pace again, her long legs eating up the ground behind the big sofa, her hair gleaming in the light.

"You're involved, Kit. You were the last person to see Inman alive, and you admitted having an argument with him. You admitted to a physical fight with him. Lord..." He wearily ran his hand through his hair. "You're a smart woman, Kit. You've run this entire ranching empire by yourself for nine years. So why can't you see that you're in trouble?"

"And why can't *you* leave me alone?"

She grimaced, as if she didn't like what she had just said. He didn't like it, either. As a matter of fact, he hated it, because he didn't have an answer. He tried to find one that made sense. "Because, Kit, you need advice of counsel. You don't realize how serious this is."

She halted and directed a level gaze at him. "Contrary to what you may think, I *do* see this as serious. Someone, while in *my* employ, has been killed on the Double B, which is *my* land. I take that very personally and will help however I can. But the sheriff needs to get his focus off me and look somewhere else."

"That's just it. He doesn't have to look somewhere else. Not if his mind is made up. And think about something else. Wouldn't it be a coup if he were to arrest the well-known Kit Baron and make it stick? The local district attorney would be drooling. The publicity would shoot them both into national prominence. There would be the possibility of book deals and interviews and maybe made-for-TV movies. It's happened before.''

"But I *didn't* do it.''

He waved dismissively. "I know you didn't.''

She blinked. "You do?''

"Kit, you're incapable of intentional cruelty *or* a cold-blooded killing.'' She was so beautiful, so stubborn. He felt an aching near his heart. He was in serious trouble. How was he going to help her when it was all he could do just to contend with the new feelings for her he had just discovered?

"Worst-case scenario,'' he said absently, trying to figure out answers to the questions he was asking himself, "we could plead self-defense.''

She picked up a vase and threw it at him as hard as she could. He ducked as it whizzed by his head and crashed against the wall behind him. "Damn you, Des Baron!''

A deafening silence descended between them, and it grew in intensity and volume until Des wanted to put his hands over his ears to drown it out. Instead, he fought to regain his composure.

"You know,'' he said calmly, "if anyone but me had seen you throw that vase, they might just believe you could lose your temper at a man who made you angry, maybe even do him bodily injury. Maybe even kill him.''

He saw her shudder as if a cold chill had slid down her spine. At last one of his points had hit home.

"Get out," she said softly.

"I'll leave. For now."

Three

Des.

Kit groaned softly. For the last ten minutes she had been rereading a paragraph in a romantic suspense book she had started earlier in the week, and she still didn't have a clue what it was about.

She thrust it aside. It was useless to try to concentrate on anything tonight. Des was the only thing on her mind, and she couldn't get him off.

All her instincts were shouting at her that earlier this morning, with very little effort, her encounter with Des could have turned from anger to passion. And if it had...

The potential for instant passion between them had always been the thing that, deep down, she had feared. Yet for some odd reason, the charged sexual tension between them had taken her totally by surprise.

It had seemed to take Des by surprise, too, though she couldn't really be sure. She couldn't begin to guess. His father had understood him, but since Uncle William's death, she doubted anyone did. He was a brilliant enigma.

She pushed herself up from the couch and walked to a window. Outside, sleet had begun to fall, but inside her home, it was warm and cozy, just as she liked. But tonight, even the surroundings she had worked so hard to achieve couldn't soothe her.

So much had happened today that was awful and bewildering. Someone had killed Cody, and the sheriff was looking closely at her as the person who had done it. If it wasn't such a bizarre tragedy, she might have laughed. Even funnier, stranger, was the fact that Des, whom she had avoided for years, had declared himself her lawyer, her defender.

She could cope with the sheriff, but Des was a different matter. She could well understand why for years women had made fools of themselves over him. At seventeen, she would have made a complete fool out of herself if he hadn't stopped their kiss. She groaned at her thoughts.

She had wrapped up business earlier this evening and treated herself to a long soak in a bath. Then she had slipped on a pair of big socks, a pair of silk pajamas and her cashmere robe. It would have been a perfect night to relax, perhaps even finish the novel she was reading, except she couldn't get her mind off the murder. And Des.

Des.

If he had kissed her this morning, she would have responded. She knew it in her bones. She wouldn't have been able to control herself. Worse, her response would have been so easy, so automatic, so natural. And what if it had gone even farther?

If nothing else, her musings on what, in reality, was nothing more than a kiss that hadn't happened told her she had been absolutely right to avoid Des for all these years.

The doorbell chimed, startling her and breaking into her thoughts. For a moment she simply gazed toward the sound. No matter who it was, she was in no mood to see anyone. She would love to simply ignore whoever was there, along with whatever problem they were bringing with them. Unfortunately, it wasn't in her to shirk any kind of responsibility.

Reluctantly, she went to answer it and found Des standing under the light on her porch. Her heart leapt, and her hand flew to the neck of her robe, pulling it tight in a protective gesture.

She had been thinking of Des and he had appeared. Slivers of ice coated his dark hair and the shoulders of his long fleece-lined coat.

Staring at him, a painful truth hit her. She had been waiting for him. Oh, Lord. Her heart shouldn't beat this fast every time he was near. Her pulse shouldn't race. She couldn't let it happen. She didn't know if he planned for them to spend a great amount of time together. But even if they spent only a small amount of time with each other, she was going to have to build a formidable defense against him.

"May I come in?"

She hesitated. "It's very late."

"Not that late."

She gave in much too easily and gestured him inside. Standing back, she watched as he shrugged out of his coat and hung it on a brass tree, then walked into the living room. She followed. The jeans he was wearing looked newer than the pair he'd had on this morning, but they still hugged every line of his hips and his long lower body. A soft-looking navy blue sweater stretched across his wide shoulders and chest and hugged his lean midriff. She could smell leather and spice and soap.

He looked wonderful. And disconcertingly desirable. "Has something happened?"

"Nothing new, if that's what you mean."

"Then why are you here?"

He glanced at her, then slowly turned his attention to the room, taking in everything about it. "This is nice," he said at last. "I didn't notice it earlier."

No, he hadn't. *Earlier* he had been concentrating very hard on her. "Thank you."

"I had heard you gutted the house and redid everything inside it."

"Yes."

He hadn't told her why he was there, which she considered a bad sign. If she knew what was coming, she could defend herself better. However, by focusing on her home, he was giving her a temporary reprieve from whatever was on his mind, and she took it.

She had decorated everything in the softest of colors, with pillows and books piled everywhere. It was her private refuge, a refuge he had invaded. And, damn it, just her luck, he looked right at home there.

His long fingers flicked at a gold tassel on a tall pillow, trailed over a soft leather chair; then his hand closed around a porcelain figurine of a woman in eighteenth-century dress and lifted it. It was so delicate he easily could have broken it, yet he held it carefully, examining its graceful lines with obvious appreciation.

Those same fingers had gripped her arms and pulled her against him.

Suddenly she had trouble swallowing. "Can I get you something? Bourbon? Scotch?" She didn't want him to stay long enough to have a drink, but, unfortunately, *she* wanted one.

"A brandy, please." He put the figurine down and strolled over to the fireplace. Holding his hands to the blaze, he remarked, "Dad told me you had redone the place, but I haven't been here in years."

She had never invited him into her home. She rarely invited anyone, though one or both of her sisters would occasionally stay a couple of days.

From the mantel, he picked up a delicate porcelain box with pink and yellow roses on its lid, gazed at it as if he didn't know how it had gotten into his hand, then put it down again. "The house is unrecognizable from your father's day. I remember a series of dark, boxy rooms—very plain, very small, very basic.''

''Yes.'' She'd knocked down walls and added windows and doors. She'd wanted the wind to be able to blow through the rooms and the light to be able to fill them. And she had succeeded. Now her home nourished her.

''I understand why you wanted to make it your own.''

Of course he did. Growing up as close as he had, he wouldn't have been able to miss the oppressive, rigid way her father had reared her and her sisters. But she wished with everything she had that he didn't understand. It made her feel too vulnerable. She poured her own drink, then sloshed a bare half-inch of brandy into a snifter and handed it to him.

''Actually, I wouldn't have been surprised if you had razed the house to the ground.''

''Doing it this way was just as effective.'' She sipped at her own brandy, then returned the glass to the bar. She had thought the brandy would help her nerves and relax her tight throat. It didn't. Since he had arrived, her nerves had tightened to the point that she was now afraid the drink might make her sick.

''I'd say it was better.''

She thought about that. ''I suppose so. I took what my father had built and recreated something bright, clean and healthy in its place. There's absolutely nothing left of the man who built it.''

''Good for you,'' he murmured.

The softness of his voice grated along her skin and

warmed her stomach. She pulled her robe tighter around her.

His gaze dropped to his brandy snifter. "Were you able to make arrangements to get Dia back all right?"

They had talked about the house, and now they were talking about her horse. As long as they weren't talking about the sexual tension that was between them, she would be okay. "I took a trailer out and got him."

One corner of his mouth turned up. "Didn't trust him to anyone else, huh?"

"Not really. Then I had to put him in a different barn than the one he's used to." Her gaze lingered on his lips entirely too long. She crossed to the fire and nudged the burning logs with a poker. "He's not happy, but for the moment, there's no other option."

She was doing the same thing as he was, she realized. She was trying to soothe the tense, heated air with small talk. The problem was, she wasn't any good at it. Neither was he.

"I talked to the sheriff this afternoon," Des said. He's conducting a very thorough forensic investigation, but he should be through with the barn by tomorrow afternoon."

"I know. He called here and told me. He also insisted again that I come in for fingerprinting."

"I don't want you to have to do that."

"I told him I would be in sometime tomorrow."

His gaze cut to her, and he exhaled a long breath. "I don't want you to do that."

"It would only antagonize the sheriff further if I

didn't. Besides, by going ahead and getting it over with, it shows I'm willing to cooperate." She paused, then finally asked, "Des, what are you doing here?"

"I thought we should settle what we started this morning."

Her nerves jumped. "I don't think there's any need to say anything more."

He set his snifter on a nearby table. "I totally disagree with you. There's every need. To start with, I lost my professional objectivity with you, something that's nearly unforgivable, considering my profession."

Oddly, she felt insulted. The term *professional objectivity* made her feel like a client with no personal ties to him, and, strangely, she resented it. However, a large dose of objectivity about him was exactly what *she* needed. She just wished she could figure out how to achieve it. "I'm sure you've already gotten it back."

He gazed at her for a long moment, and she found herself holding her breath. He affected her way too much. He always had.

"The truth is, I was worried about you, Kit. I still am."

"Don't be. There's no reason. And there's also no need for any more lectures. I've thought it over, and I fully comprehend the gravity of what's going on and how it involves me."

He nodded. "Good. I've already begun an investigation."

"You don't have to. I'll be doing my own."

"Kit..." He paused, seeming to consider carefully what he was about to say. "Do you remember when you were a little girl?"

"I try very hard not to."

He gave a chuckle that sent a warm tingle down her spine.

"Well, *I* remember," he said softly. "When your father would start to thunder at you and it all got too much for you, you used to run away from the house. After a couple of hours, your father would send the hands out to look for you. But somehow I always knew where to find you. You'd be up in the loft of one of the barns, at the very back, curled up behind a hay bale."

She tried to remember the frightened child she had been instead of the sexual woman she had become, but failed when she suddenly realized he was in front of her—too close. She hadn't even seen him move.

"You'd be curled up in a tight ball," he murmured, "trying your best to be invisible. I'd hold out my hand to you, but you'd shake your head. I'd tell you that it would be much better if you'd let me take you back to your house. I figured it would go easier on you if you returned voluntarily. But you were so stubborn. You always had to do it the hard way—your way—and you'd never accept my help."

Gently he closed his hand in her hair. "Please, Kit. This time, don't do it the hard way. This time let me help you."

Dazed, confused, she stared up at him. With that

soft mesmerizing voice, and that gentle, fiery touch, he was an extremely dangerous man.

Damn it.

"I can do this by myself, Des."

"I know that, but with me here, there's no reason for you to have to. Come on, Kit, I'm one of the highest priced lawyers in the nation, and I'm offering you my services free. I'm experienced. I'm damn good. I can help. *Let me.*"

With a sigh, she looked up at him. "You're not really going to give me a choice, are you?"

"Not really."

She slowly nodded. "Okay, then. Just to show you that I've actually learned something since I was a little girl, you can help. But if at any time during our investigation I feel we're not getting along, I can tell you to leave. Understood?"

"Good," he said simply. "Good."

His eyes dropped to her lips, then slowly, hesitantly, he lowered his face toward hers.

She had time to pull away, actually plenty of time. But she surprised herself by not moving. Instead she waited for, anticipated, what would happen next. And by doing so, she was going against everything she believed.

Still she waited, and then her waiting was over. It was as if he didn't give a second's thought to what she had said. It certainly didn't seem to faze him. His warm, soft breath feathered over her skin. She lifted her face as if the warmth was a benediction. Then, exquisitely, his lips brushed back and forth over hers.

Automatically, it seemed, her mouth opened and his tongue pushed inside. A thrill jolted through her. She thrust her tongue against his, feeling his tongue's moist roughness, tasting its sweetness, savoring the sensuality.

His hands slid up and down her spine, moving the cashmere of her robe and the silk of her pajamas over her skin in an erotic caress. One kiss turned into two, and two into three, and the kisses went on and on.

Warmth crawled along her bloodstream until it enveloped her entire body. Soon, insidiously, it changed to blazing heat. It felt so good, so wonderful, that she vaguely wondered why she had tried so hard to deprive herself all these years. Oh, she knew she had a reason, a sure belief that she should stay away from him. But at this moment, it didn't seem to matter. Truthfully, she had never known kisses could be so all-encompassing, so totally absorbing.

She melted against him, just as she had when she was seventeen. Except... The fire was somehow hotter now, the blaze inside her stronger, his lips more firm and sure. Again his tongue plunged deeply into her mouth, and she slid her arms around his neck and threaded her hands up into his thick hair.

On some level she knew these kisses went far beyond what she should be allowing, but the compulsion to continue was much too strong to stop now.

She pressed her body closer to his, shamelessly undulating her hips until she could feel the hard ridge of his arousal. It was crazy. She had tried so hard for so long to stay away from him, and now she couldn't get close enough.

Gently, firmly, he pushed her away, making space between their bodies.

An involuntary cry of protest and denial escaped her lips. "Ah, don't make that sound," he murmured, his voice hoarse and broken. "It hurts me, too. But if we continue this much longer, I won't be able to stop."

The reality of what he was saying cleared her head. One part of her wanted to sink back into the heat where she didn't have to think and feel. The other part of her, which was now thinking straighter, knew that there were innumerable things wrong with them continuing.

Suddenly she felt as if she had been put through an emotional wringer, and weariness rapidly overwhelmed her. Without meeting his eyes, she stepped away. "Good night, Des."

He hesitated. "I didn't mean for—"

"Good night."

"You want me to go?" he asked stiffly.

"That's exactly what I want."

"Then good night, Kit."

Four

Des.

The next morning, Kit pulled back the drape of the living room window and gazed outside. It promised to be raw and gray all day.

Earlier, she had taken Dia out for their run, but, unlike yesterday, she hadn't been tempted to lengthen their time away from home. Today's run hadn't brought her problems into focus as it usually did, nor had it cleared her mind.

Des dominated her thoughts at a time when it was imperative she should be thinking of Cody's murder and how to help herself. It was no solace to her that she had been right all these years to avoid him. He could so easily fill her life to the exclusion of everything else. He could dominate her as her father had done, and she wouldn't even be tempted to run away.

She was angry at herself for having been so easy, and she knew that everything that had happened between them had been her fault. She had known the kiss was coming, and she should have said no.

Don't think about it, she ordered herself.

Easier said than done, she answered herself.

She was really losing it, she reflected ruefully.

She forced her thoughts back to Cody's murder. She didn't know anything about this sheriff. Des had said he was ambitious. To her way of thinking, it would be odd if he wasn't.

But if he *was* looking for a quick, expedient end to this case, circumstances had unwittingly made her the perfect solution. And because of that, any clues he would be looking for would be clues that linked her to the murder. He wouldn't be interested in anything or anyone else.

Des had been right. The innocent person didn't always go free. Oh, maybe in books and the movies, but not in real life.

But the last thing she wanted was for Des to help her.

She did not want to be beholden to him. Plus, last night had proven to her that she couldn't keep her head when she was around him. She had lost her temper. She had melted when he had touched her. She had made a fool of herself.

Briefly she closed her eyes. Somehow she was going to have to gain control over both herself and the situation with him. She was going to have to help herself.

If she hadn't killed Cody, someone else had. But who?

Last night, after Des had left, she had turned on her computer, opened a file and checked the reports of every one of her managers. Finally, she had found the one who had overseen Cody. A quick call on the man's pager resulted in a callback and the information that a man named Scott McKee frequently worked and hung out with Cody.

The doorbell rang, and she went to greet him. "Good morning, Scott."

He was a young man, still in his twenties, around five feet ten inches tall, with a stocky, muscular build. He swept off his hat to reveal the beginnings of a receding hairline. "Ms. Baron."

She had been in a group several times with him, and he had always called her Kit, but she didn't ask him to call her Kit now. This morning there was a definite formality to his demeanor and to the occasion.

"Let's go to my office."

She led the way down the hall to the big room that overlooked the back garden. She took her chair behind her desk and, with a wave of her hand, indicated that he should sit in one of the chairs in front of her. "Coffee?" She pointed toward a sideboard, a coffeepot and a stack of mugs she had previously set out. He shook his head, clearly uncomfortable in his surroundings.

"Then I'll get right to the point, Scott. I'd like to know about your friendship with Cody Inman. Were you close?"

He shifted awkwardly in the chair. "I wouldn't say we had what you'd call a real friendship. Depending on where we were each assigned, we'd sometimes work together. We bunked fairly close, too."

The first thing on her mind had been to get him settled so that she could begin questioning him, but now she studied his face. He looked uneasy and apprehensive.

"Did you ever hang out with him when you weren't working?"

"Once in a while. Damned shame he was killed."

"I'm not just sorry about his death, Scott. I'm angry. I value every person who works on this ranch, whether I know them well or not."

She paused, but he had started to studiously examine the near edge of the desk and didn't say anything.

"Someone committed murder here. Until we find out who, other people could be in danger."

"I hadn't thought about it like that."

"But it's true."

"Yes, ma'am."

"Did you have reason to be mad at Cody recently?"

He looked at her. "No. Did you?"

She returned his look as calmly as she could manage. News traveled fast on the ranch. By now he knew what had happened between her and Cody. By now everyone did.

Scott retreated into silence, and her heart sank. Scott was feeling awkward with her because he thought it possible she had killed Cody. Did others feel the same way?

Something in her screamed.

This ranch and her place on it were her pride and joy. This ranch was all that she had, all that she wanted. And the respect of each and every person who worked on the ranch was something she valued highly. Now she saw that with some she might have to work hard to regain that respect.

"Do you know of anyone who didn't get along with Cody? Anyone he fought with recently? Anyone who didn't like him?"

He shrugged, glanced at her, then returned his gaze to the edge of the desk. "Not really."

"Think hard."

"The thing is, he was pretty much a regular guy. Nothing too special about him. He worked hard And when he played, he played hard." His voice dropped. "Just like we all do, I guess."

He was thinking of her, and it was one more reason to find out who really had killed Cody.

"Good morning," Des said, walking into the room, taking it over with his forceful, magnetic presence.

Scott immediately straightened. "Mr. Baron."

Des dropped down into one of the other chairs and looked at her. "Morning, Kit."

She nodded stiffly, losing her train of thought. "I didn't expect you."

"I just thought I'd drop by." He turned to Scott. "I don't think we've met. I'm Des Baron."

"Yes, sir. I know who you are. I'm Scott McKee."

"Scott sometimes hung out with Cody," she inserted by way of explanation.

"Good, then don't let me interrupt. Go on with what you were doing and I'll just listen."

Continuing with what she had been doing was easier said than done. With Des in the room, it was hard to remember there was anybody else there. Des had a personality that was difficult to ignore, and she didn't think she felt that way just because she was inexplicably drawn to him. A glance at Scott told her that Des was having the same effect on him. No matter how one regarded Des, he was a force. In some ways he could be like a Texas tornado, knocking down everything that stood in his way.

With one more look at Des, she returned her attention to Scott. "Did you see Cody night before last or yesterday morning?"

The younger man shifted in his chair, obviously miserable at being in the spotlight. "There was a late night pickup game of poker. I saw him then."

She inched forward in her chair. "You mean *after* he and I came back?"

His gaze shifted to his knee. "Cody did mention something about being out with you."

She just bet he had. He had probably been bragging. *Damn it.* She couldn't forgive herself for having such lousy judgment.

"Was he one of the players?" Des asked quietly.

"Yeah."

"Were you?"

"I dropped out when he came in."

"Did you stay, though?"

"For a while, then I left."

"Did anyone lose big after Cody came in?"

"Not that I can remember. The stakes weren't that high, not like right after payday."

She reached for her pen. "Give me the names of everyone who was there."

Scott hesitated momentarily, as if he was considering whether or not he was about to betray someone. Thankfully he apparently decided he wasn't and reeled off the names of five players.

"Well, there was Cody, of course. Then Mike Stillwell, Red Tinsdall, Scooter Garner, Burt Salatore and Johnny Don Galvez."

She wrote the names down. "Is there anything else you'd like to tell me?"

Scott shook his head.

"Then thanks. I appreciate it."

Scott surged to his feet. "That's all?"

She nodded. "That's it. You can get back to work now."

He couldn't get out the door fast enough. At any other time Kit would have laughed. Instead she turned to her computer and quickly input the names of the men he had given her. Then she sat back and waited while the files printed out.

"I meant to ask you last night," Des said. "Are your fingerprints on file anywhere?"

She looked over at him. "No."

He nodded. "Fingerprints aren't really what the sheriff is after, anyway. He knows that getting your fingerprints isn't going to do him a lot of good, so he's using them as an excuse."

"What for?"

"I've made a couple more phone calls about the man, and it seems he's big on intimidation. What he really wants is to get you into his office, where you'll be on his turf. Then he'll have you go over and over the story, hoping that if you tell it enough times, and he asks the same questions in different ways, you'll eventually trip yourself up and reveal that you killed Cody."

"Then he's in for a disappointment."

He smiled, and it was one of the most brilliant smiles she had ever seen him give. She felt as if she had just been struck by lightning. How on earth was she supposed to ignore a smile like that?

"So what's your plan? What are you going to do first?" he asked.

"I'm going to find these five men and talk to them."

"Then let's go."

"That's not—"

He raised his hand. "I really want to come with

you. As your counsel, I'll be helping you to make the case that you're innocent.''

So his reason for wanting to come with her wasn't personal. She should learn from him. She turned back to the computer and punched in more commands.

"What are you doing now?"

"I'm accessing my managers' reports that tell which employee works under them, when and where each employee worked on a given day, and what they accomplished."

He chuckled. "If there's one certainty on a ranch, it's that conditions can change at any given moment, sending the ranch hands off in an entirely different direction for an entirely different task."

She nodded, taking in the deep, warm sound of his laugh. "I get the reports at the end of each week. I haven't yet received this week's reports, but last week's will give us a place to start."

Us. She had said *us.* She desperately needed to erect a formidable barrier against him, but unfortunately, one chuckle, one smile, one twinkle in his eyes, and she was wondering what it would be like to kiss him again. She quietly sighed. After this whole mess was over, and he left, she would definitely put him out of her mind.

They found Bill Ridley, one of her managers, fairly easily. He was at one of the big hay barns, supervising several men who were unloading a flatbed of hay.

Bill had worked on the ranch ever since she could remember. According to his file, he was fifty-three years old. His dark hair already held slivers of silver, and he had a belly that hung over his handtooled belt. To her relief, he seemed genuinely delighted to see her. Obviously he wasn't one of the ones who thought she could have killed Cody.

"Kit, Des, it's great to see you."

Des shook his hand. "Good to see you, too. It's been a while."

"Sure has." Bill's gaze flitted between them. "What are you two doing out this way?"

Kit spoke up. "I need some information on Cody Inman."

Bill's grin faded. "Damn shame about his murder. I almost couldn't believe it. Fistfights are a common enough occurrence. Sometimes a man can get beat half to death before the fight is broken up, but I don't think we've ever had a murder on the Double B."

She nodded. "I've sure never heard of a murder, though who knows what happened in the early days."

"You're right about that. It was pretty rough-and-tumble back then."

"I can well imagine." She handed him her hand-written list of names. "Listen, my records indicate these men have been working under you. I need to find out what shift they're working and where they are."

He glanced at the list. "Any reason I should know?"

"No. It's just that they were all at a poker game two nights ago with Cody, and I just thought it might be good to talk to them. Can you help me?"

"Sure thing. Got the assignments in my pickup over there." He quickly walked to his truck, pulled out a clipboard, then returned. "Okay, well, let's see. Burt and Red are up on NW Section 258, checking out the herd for me. They'll be there for a few days. As for Mike, he left at first light for Oklahoma and his sister's funeral." He flipped to another sheet; then, using his finger, he scanned it. "Oh, right. I sent Scooter and Johnny Don up to Oklahoma City to pick up a special order. I expect 'em back tomorrow." He looked at her. "Is that any help?"

"It's a great help. Thanks. I just want to touch base with these men as quickly as I can and see what they can remember. Now that I know where they are, I can arrange my schedule accordingly."

"Good idea. Be sure and let me know if you need anything else."

"I will."

His good humor returned. "Hey, Des, how long you home for this time?"

"Indefinitely."

"You're *kidding*."

"No."

"Hey, that's great news."

Kit started, sharing Bill's surprise and then some. Des was never home for long; he usually stayed only a few days. But now he was staying *indefinitely?*

If Des noticed her surprise, he didn't show it. "Yeah, I've decided not to take on any more cases, at least for a while. I'm going to do a little consulting from here. The computer age has provided us with instant communication, and I've decided to give it a try."

"Well, it'll be good to have you home."

Des smiled. "I agree. I miss the Double B when I stay away too long."

"Before we start out to find them, I need to stop by my office and pick up the men's files." Kit was a bit amazed at herself for forgetting something so basic. Agitated, nervous, she finger-combed her hair away from her face. "I can't believe I went off without them in the first place."

"You've had a lot on your mind," Des murmured, turning his truck toward her house.

"Yeah, I guess so." What an understatement, she reflected. "So when were you going to tell me about your decision to start working from the ranch? Or did you plan to just let me figure it out gradually when you didn't leave?"

"I would have told you at the appropriate time. It's just that since Cody's death, we've had…other things to talk about."

Another understatement. "Yes, we certainly have."

Something in her voice must have drawn his attention. He looked over at her. "It's getting to you, isn't it?"

"Of course it is. I don't see how it could be otherwise. It's not every day I'm suspected of murder, you know."

"Would it help if I promised you that you've got nothing to worry about?"

A promise was an intangible thing, but instinctively she knew that a man like Des wouldn't make one lightly. The fact that he had meant he felt he could back it up. The thought made her feel good, which wasn't good at all. She was putting her trust in someone other than herself, something that over the years she had schooled herself not to do.

She deliberately pushed the thought aside and returned to his astounding decision. "Sure," she said casually, then changed the subject. "So when did you make the decision to stay home?"

"It's something I've been thinking about for a while."

"But it's such a radical decision. Have you considered the very real possibility that you may miss the excitement of trial law?"

"Sure, but I've had that excitement. After a while, it gets old."

"So does everything."

"Not everything. For instance, you can't tell me that you ever find life on the Double B old."

A grin broke out on her face before she could censor it. "No chance. Every day is different."

He smiled. "Exactly. And I love the ranch, just like you do. I wasn't born here, but my roots are here. I don't feel truly at home any other place."

If she had ever given the matter a moment's thought, she might have realized that he would feel that way. Still…what was it going to mean to her to have him living on the ranch all the time?

For one thing, avoiding him was going to be much more difficult, maybe impossible. And there was something else bothering her. She had always considered the ranch *her* domain and hers alone. Thankfully her sisters' interests had always lain elsewhere. "You need to know that *I* run the Double B, and that I definitely don't need anyone else's help."

He chuckled. "That's such a *Kit* thing to say."

"Are you saying I'm predictable?"

He laughed. "*Never.* In fact, I'd be a complete fool to say that."

She shook her head. "You could never be a fool." She had never thought she could be one, either, but because of last night, she had changed her mind.

"Thank you. And just to ease your mind, let me state for the record that I have no plans to so much as stick a finger into the running of the ranch. I think I said it before. You're doing an excellent job."

"But since you now own fifty percent of Baron International, you are legally entitled."

"I know."

"And you just told me you loved the ranch."

"I do. But I wouldn't like to run it. All the details would keep me from enjoying it."

"The details are fun."

Humor glinted in his eyes. "Now you sound as if you're trying to talk me into helping you run it."

Lord help her, he was right, and it was just another

sign of how mixed up she was. "Okay, so then what *are* you going to do here?"

"Basically, give myself the luxury of time."

"I still don't understand."

"I'm going to enjoy being home, Kit." He pulled the truck to a stop in front of her house. "Looks like we've got company."

Her next question to him died in her throat. The sheriff's car was parked alongside a van with *The Courier* emblazoned on its side. It was the name of a local newspaper. "What's going on?"

"I'm not sure, but let's go find out. Just remember to be careful of what you say, and when in doubt, let me do the talking."

She almost smiled. "I think we've been over that ground before."

"Who won?"

She chuckled. "You did, but there'll be no argument over this. I'll handle it."

Five

——

"Hello, Sheriff Moreno," Kit said in greeting. "Are you here to conduct more forensics testing?"

The sheriff glanced at Des, then back at her. "I have someone handling that as we speak, and we're also still searching for the murder weapon."

"Good. I sincerely hope you'll be able to find something that will help you."

"Oh, I'm positive I will."

His tone registered as sarcastic, but she decided not to rise to the bait. She gestured to her house. "So why are you here and not down at the barn?"

"Ordinarily I would be, but in your case, I decided it would be best to drive out and escort you into town for your fingerprinting."

He had just insulted her. Beside her, she felt Des stiffen. "I already told you that I would come in sometime today."

He shrugged. "There was always the possibility that you might forget. I thought I'd better make sure you didn't."

"You're way out of line, Moreno." Des spoke quietly, but a vein beat prominently at his temple.

The sheriff cut his gaze to him. "I disagree."

"Then you're wrong."

"What I *am,* Mr. Baron, is *thorough.*"

The smile that touched Des's mouth held no humor. "Actually, what you *are* is a whole other conversation best saved for another day. For now, I will just tell you that Ms. Baron is not going anywhere with you at this time unless you are prepared to arrest her."

"I seriously doubt if that's really what you want me to do." Something close to a smirk formed on the sheriff's face.

"You know damned well you can't arrest her. You don't have enough evidence."

"That's debatable."

"Then we'll debate it in court."

Sheriff Moreno's chin came up. "Later, perhaps. But for now, let's just say that I'm extending a *courtesy* to Ms. Baron."

"Call it what you will, but for now, leave this property. Ms. Baron will drive into town in a timely manner."

"Which could mean anything at all."

Up to that point, Kit had been fairly neutral on the sheriff's behavior, but now she realized she actively disliked him. What was more, Des was very close to losing his fabled composure. She put a staying hand on his arm. "Let me speak for myself."

"Excellent idea, and just why I'm here," a smooth female voice said.

Kit looked around at the woman who had been standing off to one side. She had almost forgotten there was somebody else there, but now she remembered the newspaper van.

"Hello, Ms. Baron. I'm Ada de la Garza." The petite woman had her dark hair swept up into a tight French twist and wore a camera-flattering red wool suit, though there were no cameras in site.

Kit eyed the business card the woman presented to her. "A reporter."

"That's right. And I plan to do a story on everything that has been going on out here."

"You mean the murder?"

Ms. de la Garza smiled broadly and, with a flourish, produced a notebook and pen. "Exactly. Hello, Mr. Baron. It's so nice to meet you." Her gaze was openly flirtatious. "I'm sorry, though, for the circumstances. Perhaps when this whole unfortunate mess is over we can meet again."

With hidden amusement Kit looked at Des expectantly. He had cut his teeth on women like Ada and knew just how to handle her.

He smiled charmingly. "I'm afraid my schedule is always packed, and that's just the way I like it."

He had left Ms. de la Garza with no place to go, yet he hadn't been cruel. Kit not only applauded his method, she realized she would have been upset if he had shown even a small amount of interest in the woman.

"I see." Ms. de la Garza appeared slightly dented yet nevertheless determined. She returned her attention to Kit. "Ms. Baron, our readers deserve to know every detail of the circumstances surrounding the murder of Cody Inman. For instance, I understand the two of you were seen dancing at a bar the night before the murder. Was the affair between you serious?"

"No—"

"And how long had that affair been going on?"

"We weren't having an affair. That was the first—"

"Oh, you were at the *start* of the affair." As the woman made notes, she fired another quick question at Kit. "Tell me, Ms. Baron, what was it about Cody Inman that got past that famous princess-of-all-you-survey attitude of yours and suddenly made all your other men fade into the background?"

Kit didn't know which outrageous remark to respond to first. "What *other* men?"

The red lipstick on Ada de la Garza's wide mouth gleamed as she smiled knowingly. "Oh, please. Now's not the time to play coy. Obviously the man had something that attracted your attention. For instance, he must have been good-looking, right? Perhaps with that cowboy sort of machismo that most of the men out here seem to have."

"I don't know what you're talking about," Kit said flatly.

"Oh, come on. You know exactly what I'm talking about. After all, you're a woman who's obviously *very* aware of men. You work day in and day out surrounded by them. What could be more glorious for a woman like you? The temptations must be enormous, and you're certainly no angel."

Kit was horrified at the woman's perception of her. Where on earth had it come from? She glanced at the sheriff, and something about his smug expression told her that he had tipped off the reporter. If de la Garza wrote the story using the prejudicial things she had said to her so far, it would play right into what the sheriff wanted.

She looked back at the woman. "Why are you saying those things? You and I have never even met."

"But I've seen you around. Everyone has. You have a way of making sure you're noticed."

"I beg your pardon?"

Des firmly clasped Kit's arm. "Ms. de la Garza, if you want an interview, then call for an appointment." He tugged Kit toward the house and fell into step beside her.

The reporter followed them. "How about an interview right now, Kit? I'm here. You're here. And there's no time like the present."

Kit didn't know which she hated more—the woman's familiar use of her name, or the idea of her personal life becoming public property to be talked about over the breakfast tables of people she had never even met. "I don't think so."

"Come on, Kit. You know I'm going to write the story with or without your help."

The woman was rude and abrasive. And she was also blatantly unsympathetic to her. One reason could be that she had the look of a woman who saw all other women as competition. But the better explanation would be that trashy stories with juicy details were always top sellers. Still, the woman had given her a glimpse of how other people must see her, and her confidence was shaken.

"Kit, did you hear what I said? Call me."

"Call for an appointment," Des repeated to the reporter, opening the front door.

"It won't be an accurate story unless Kit gives me her side."

"Then don't write it." Without another word, Des ushered Kit into the house.

With a barely muffled groan, she headed straight for the couch in the living room, sank down onto it and buried her face in her hands.

Des sat down beside her and hung a loose arm around her shoulder. "Don't let that woman get to you. She's simply not worth it."

"Something about her scares me, Des."

"That's understandable. She's a predator, and you're sensing it, that's all."

Kit scrubbed her face with her hands. "A predator disguised in a smart red suit with the ear of the public and using our constitution's First Amendment as a weapon. That makes her a *powerful* predator.''

''Ignore her.''

''I'd love to, but I'm not sure she's going to let me. And what am I going to say to her when she comes after me again? That I refuse to answer on the grounds that it might incriminate me? Good grief, just saying those words makes me sound guilty.''

''As long as this case is open, you can't be faulted for trying to protect yourself. And saying that is well within your right.''

She looked over at him. ''You're talking like a lawyer.''

He smiled softly. ''We've agreed that I'm *your* lawyer, remember? And even if we hadn't, speaking like a lawyer is a hard habit to break, particularly when it involves someone I care about.''

He had just said he cared about her. It was an extraordinary statement, but most likely made to reassure her that she would come out on the other end of this nightmare whole and well. She prayed he was right, but she wasn't reassured.

''You know,'' she said slowly, ''I had no idea so many people thought so badly of me.''

''You heard that from *one* person, Kit. *One*. Moreover, she's a person who's out to get something from you. She wants the fame she thinks she'll get if she exploits you.'' His tone turned disgusted. ''She and the sheriff have that in common.''

The fact that he was right didn't lessen the impact

the reporter's words had had on her. If anything, it meant the woman would do her worst.

He pulled her closer to him. "Kit, since you were old enough to be aware of your circumstances and the people around you, you've known that you had to be cautious of everyone in case it was just your name and fortune they were attracted to."

She gave a hollow laugh. "And most of the time it was exactly those two things they were attracted by."

"I'm sure there were many who fell into that category. I had more than my share of that type trying to hang around me, too. But along the way you've managed to make many true friends. I know that for a fact. Plus, you have your sisters and—"

She shook her head. "We're not close."

"That's not their fault. There's nothing they'd like better than to be close to you. And I know without a doubt that they'd be here for you on a moment's notice if they knew you were in trouble."

Her eyes widened in dread. "You won't tell them, will you?"

"I'd like to. I think you could use their support."

"Des, no!"

"Okay. If you don't want me to contact them, I won't."

"Please don't. And don't let it slip to their husbands, either. I know you talk to them." She couldn't think of anything worse than having her sisters hovering around her, feeling sorry for her.

"Fine. But have you considered that when de la

Garza's first article hits the paper, it will more than likely be picked up around the state, perhaps even the nation? Your sisters are bound to hear of it sooner or later.''

"I'll deal with that when and if it happens." Lately she seemed to be putting off facing quite a bit. She relaxed her body against his and pressed her face against his chest. She didn't fully realize what she had done until she inhaled her first breath of him—spice, leather, sensuality. All in all, he was a man she was getting much too close to.

Another time the idea would have alarmed her so much that she would have pulled away. But right at that moment she felt a bottomless need to be comforted, and his warmth and strength were doing just that.

So she stayed right where she was. He didn't say anything more, and she didn't, either. And while he held her, time and her worries were suspended.

Kit dialed her sister Tess's number, then sat back and waited. She didn't know when she had decided to call her sisters. She just knew that one minute she was telling Des not to contact them and the next *she* was doing it. At the moment Tess was in Austin, where her husband, Nick Trejo, was a professor of archaeology at the University of Texas.

"Tess, this is Kit."

"Well, *hi*. This is a surprise."

She didn't doubt it. She could count on the fingers

of one hand the times she had called either of her sisters lately.

"A *pleasant* one though," Tess hastened to add. "How are you?"

"I'm okay." She had tried to think of a way to ease into the news, but she hadn't been able to, so she simply told her. "Listen, there's something you should know. Something has happened here. I'm afraid one of the ranch hands has been murdered."

"Oh, Kit, how awful. Did I know him?"

"No. He had been with us less than a year."

"Who did it?"

"No one knows at this point, but for whatever reason, the sheriff thinks I did—or at least he's trying to prove I did."

"You've got to be kidding."

"Believe me, I wish I was."

"But why *you?*"

Kit proceeded to lay out everything for her sister, telling her exactly what had happened and, for good measure, including the part about Ada de la Garza. She left out only those things that had occurred between Des and her that might be construed as remotely personal. How could she give her those details? She hadn't yet come to terms with them herself.

"Thank goodness Des was home," Tess said. "I know he's being a big help."

Kit's mind wandered to the kiss they had shared. It had been helpful only in that it had taken her mind off the murder. But it had also left her terribly confused.

"Kit?"

"Oh, I'm sorry. Yes, he is."

"Okay, I've got one of the jets here at the airport. I'll be there by this evening."

"No, *don't*. There's honestly no need. Des and I have everything under control." She nearly stumbled over the words. "As a matter of fact, I'm waiting for him now. We're about to go out and interview a couple of the men who were playing poker with Cody the night before he was murdered."

"Are you sure? Because I'd really like to help. I mean, if nothing else, I could field calls, hold your hand…whatever is needed."

"No, I'm positive. I just wanted to let you know what was going on here. I wanted you to be prepared in case you were told about it before it's resolved."

"I'm glad you did. Have you told Jill yet?"

"I plan to call her as soon as I hang up with you."

"Kit, promise me you'll call if you need any backup or anything else. And for heaven's sakes, please keep me up-to-date on what's going on. I'll be worrying like crazy."

"Don't. Honestly, Tess, everything is going to be fine."

"You're sure you've got everything under control?"

She almost laughed in her sister's ear. "I'm positive. Bye for now."

Hanging up, she said a short prayer that she was right. Then she picked up the phone again and dialed Jill.

* * *

Later that afternoon, as Des guided his truck over the bumpy trail, Kit sat in the corner watching the snow whirl around them. They were heading for the Double B's NW Section 258 to interview Red Tinsdall and Burt Salatore, because according to manager Bill Ridley, that was the section where he had assigned them.

"I'm glad you called your sisters."

"I guess I am, too, although what I was afraid of happened. They both wanted to fly in. I had a horrible time trying to talk Jill out of it. Tess was a little easier to convince."

"Jill's pregnant. She could be feeling especially protective."

"Maybe." For a moment she allowed herself to wonder what it would be like to be pregnant with the baby of the man she loved. A yearning stirred near her heart.

"I still think we should have held off on this trip until morning," Des said, interrupting her musings. "That sky is getting lower by the minute."

"I know."

When he had come to pick her up, he had warned her that the weather looked as if it were going to turn bad and had suggested that they put off the trip until tomorrow. But the weather reports she had received that morning hadn't indicated a storm, and she hadn't been willing to wait.

"I also told the sheriff I'd come in to see him today. But I really want to talk to Red and Burt before

I do. I'm hoping they'll know something that will be helpful." She paused. "The sheriff will have to wait for his fingerprints a little longer."

"Good."

She glanced at him. "You didn't have to come."

"Yes," he said quietly. "I did. And we can still turn back. Just say the word."

"I want to keep going. The sooner we can find out who really killed Cody, the better off I'll be." *We.* Somehow she had become very familiar with using the plural when it came to the two of them. Amazing. She gazed out the window. "Besides, this truck can handle a little snow."

"Yeah, it can. A *little*. But it's steadily getting worse."

She bit back a sharp retort. He was only trying to help her, she reminded herself. "It'll be okay. We're almost there."

In fact, it was some time later before they pulled up to the line cabin, and the sun was already beginning to set. And Des had been right in his weather prediction. The snow had gotten worse.

"I can't see any sign of life."

She followed his gaze. There were no footprints in the snow anywhere, and there was no smoke coming out of the chimney. She climbed out of the truck. "The guys must still be out on the range, but I'm sure they'll be back soon."

"Then why don't you go in?" he said, already heading for the back of the cabin. "I'll bring in some wood."

"You don't want any help?" she called after him.

"Nope."

With a mental shrug, she went inside. An oil lamp hung just inside the door, and a tin of matches waited on a shelf. She lit the lamp, then held it up and gazed around, wondering if she had been in this cabin before. She had been in many of the others, and they were all pretty much the same—practical, but with an eye toward comfort.

Bunk beds lined the back wall. Several more stuck out from another wall. A potbellied stove took the place of honor in the center. There was also a kitchenette and a bathroom. It was cozy, but also very cold.

The door blew open and snow swirled. Des stamped his feet free of snow and came in. "Here we go. This place will be warm in no time." He kicked the door shut behind him, then knelt in front of the stove and began feeding it wood. "Are you hungry?"

"I don't know. To tell the truth, food has been the last thing on my mind today." She positioned the lamp on the table.

"Well, think about it now. Without even looking in the cabinets, I can tell you there'll be a variety of soups, beans and no telling what else. Ranch hands have hearty appetites." He nodded toward the kitchen. "Do you see a cooler anywhere? Sometimes a truck will come out with ice and fresh food. We might luck out."

"I'll check," she said, basically to give herself

something to do. She was too keyed up to do nothing but sit around and wait.

"And I'll go out and bring some more wood in. We may be here a while."

"I'll light a few more lamps."

She settled on thickening up several cans of soup by adding beans and then ended their ad-libbed dinner with a freshly made pot of coffee. While it was perking, Des washed their few dishes and she put them away. But the tasks were soon done, and she couldn't think of any more work to keep her busy.

"Do you still want to wait?" he asked.

Reluctant to give up at this point and go home without seeing the men, she nodded. "I'm sure they're on the way back here."

"Okay, fine." He pulled up a chair to the potbellied stove and gestured for her to sit.

She shook her head. "Go ahead." She sank down on one of the bunks.

He took the chair. "This is nice." Without a trace of self-consciousness, he leaned back and stretched his long legs out to the warmth. "I've spent a lot of evenings in different cabins on different parts of the ranch doing nothing much more than this. Sometimes I'd play dominoes or maybe read." He looked over at her. "Most kids had television to keep them entertained. I had this ranch and the people on it."

She wished she felt as content as he looked, but eating hadn't calmed her a bit, and her nerves were still stretched to the breaking point. Unfortunately, though, it wasn't because of anything involving the murder, but rather because of Des and the way just looking at him made her think of things that could, would, never be. "You obviously have a lot of good memories from growing up here."

"You bet."

She envied that. The ranch and her work gave her an incredible amount of satisfaction, but sometimes, when she wasn't careful, her bad memories would eclipse the good. "Tell me some of them."

He looked over at her. "Really?"

"Yeah. It'll be fun for me to hear a totally different viewpoint than mine of growing up here." She also needed something to distract her from the fact that the two of them were alone in an isolated cabin during a snowstorm.

"Okay, then. As it happens, I have several memories of you, and they happened in winter."

"*Me?*"

"That's right. Do you want to hear them?"

"Sure." The news that in the past she had managed to capture Des's attention in some way, even once, astounded her.

"Okay, well, let's see… Once I was driving along and happened to see you." He slowly grinned. "There you were, maybe twelve, thirteen years old, skating all alone on that frozen pond out behind Barn Twenty-six."

She blinked, trying to remember what occasion he could be talking about, but the softness on his face kept distracting her.

"You were wearing an old pair of jeans and a

faded green cable-knit sweater. And you had your hair pulled back into a ponytail.'' He chuckled. ''But as cute as that ponytail was, it couldn't begin to subdue that hair of yours.''

All at once she was intensely aware of how she looked. Jeans and a sweater was her normal uniform during the winter, and it was what she was wearing now. She reached up to push an unruly lock of hair off her face.

''Don't.'' The command was barely above a whisper, but she heard it and went still.

''Your hair is glorious. It always has been, and it always will be.''

The Des sitting across from her was one she didn't know how to cope with. Ignoring him was out of the question. And as for responding... Well, she had done that, and it had led her to a place she didn't trust herself to go again. ''Thank you,'' she murmured, wildly searching for some safe middle ground. Surely there had to be some.

He stared at her for several moments, his thoughts hidden, as they so often were. But there were his words....

Six

—————

"**Y**our movements were utterly graceful as you skated," Des said, continuing. "And heaven above, but you were beautiful—all color and motion etched against a huge, slate gray sky. For the first time in my life, but not the last, I wished I was a painter so that I could capture you like that. But frankly, I can't think of an artist who could be that good. You were all about beauty and energy that day, just like you were today." He paused. "Just like you are now."

He left her breathless, and she honestly didn't have a clue how to respond. Or even how to help herself.

"And then there was another time, when you were about fifteen or sixteen. A young steer had wandered out onto one of the frozen ponds and onto a section of thin ice. He'd fallen in, of course, and was well on his way to drowning. Except you had found him and were doing your level best to save him.''

"What was I doing?''

"Somehow you'd managed to get a rope around his neck and had the other end tied off on the saddle horn. Your horse was backing up, doing his best to pull, but that wasn't good enough for you. You were down on the ice, tugging on that rope with all your might.''

There was no reason why she would have remembered that one incident, she reflected. Living and working on the ranch over the years had required her to do many things, and when she could, she had always tried to steal time away just for herself. Yet Des had remembered it.

"It looked to me as if you were about to go into the ice with the damn cow, so I slammed on the brakes and got out, intending to race over to help you. But you were fast. Before I had even gone a foot, you had wrestled that cow and yourself onto firm ground.'' He chuckled again. "I'll never forget the look of complete and absolute determination on your face as you fought to save that animal. And I'll never forget the laugh you gave when he was safe.''

"You heard me?''

He rose and moved over to the bunk where she was. The mattress gave way as he came down beside her. "If I had ever heard you laugh before, I couldn't remember it.'' He lifted his hand and touched her hair. "And the laugh itself—there was an elation in it that was..."

His nearness shouldn't affect her so much, but it did. It seemed it always had. She could feel the air backing up in her lungs. And she shouldn't care what he was about to say next, but she did. Desperately. "Was what?"

"Memorable."

"I—I don't remember you ever being around when I was doing anything like that."

"No, you wouldn't. Both times you were completely absorbed in what you were doing. I occasionally still see that same look of absorption and determination on your face today."

"But why didn't you let me know you were there?"

He shrugged. "I guess once I knew you were safe I got caught up in watching you. Plus, now that I think about it, I'm glad I didn't."

He was bewildering her, baffling her. "Why?"

"Because back then you had this tendency of turning shy whenever I was around. It would have spoiled the moment."

He was right. If she had known he was anywhere nearby, she would have turned extremely shy. And if she had known he was *watching* her, she most likely would have become paralyzed.

"But believe me when I say to you that both times you were absolutely wonderful." His hand slipped behind her neck, and he drew her toward him. "You were wonderful then, and you are wonderful now."

She barely managed to stifle a groan. He wasn't giving her a chance. "I can't believe that."

"I know you don't. It's part of why I find you charming."

"Des, I think—"

He pressed two fingers to her lips. "In this case, I can almost read your mind."

"I hope that's not true."

He smiled. "Okay, maybe I can only read part of your mind. The part that says things nearly got out of hand between us last night, and that now, suddenly, things are different than they were the day before."

He had guessed part of it. She cleared her throat. "To be accurate, there was nothing between us last night."

"Who are you trying to kid? I was there, remember? And there was definitely something. Admit it."

A warmth began to crawl through her veins. "Okay, there was something. There was…history."

"And what's so wrong about that? History's good. It gives two people something to build on."

Frantically she looked around, trying to find something to distract both of them. "You know, I—I'm sure the guys will be back any minute."

His mouth began to drop toward hers. "On the other hand, they could have decided to drive back to the homestead."

His breath caressed her lips. "I suppose."

"Or they could even have decided to camp out so they can be close to the herd."

"Uh-huh."

His mouth settled firmly on hers, and the heat was instant. It rushed to every part of her body. Like a wildfire, it consumed everything in its path.

It shouldn't be this easy, she thought vaguely. Just because he wanted to kiss her, that didn't mean she had to kiss him back. But of their own volition her lips opened beneath his, and, accepting the unspoken invitation, his tongue darted deep into her mouth. Welcoming the invasion, she twined her tongue around his, and whatever small amount of resistance that was remaining in her began to drain away.

Something in her stomach clenched. Something near her heart turned over. Fire filled her every pore. And when his arms slipped around her and he pulled her to him, she willingly went. Everything about this moment felt so good, so right.

What was the use? She couldn't fight her feelings for Des anymore. Why even try, when everything in her was shouting that exquisite passion was hers for the asking? She wanted it, she needed it, and so she allowed herself to take it.

She flattened her palm against his chest and felt the heavy pounding of his heart. Elation soared through her. He wanted her. The knowledge gave her a new confidence.

He skinned her sweater over her head. Her bra had covered very little of her, and soon it covered nothing. With a single flick of his fingers, the beige lace undergarment fell away, and in the next instant his hand was covering her breast.

In a distant part of her mind she heard a moan. It

took her a moment before she realized the sound was
her own voice. It was a measure of how much he was
affecting her that she hadn't recognized it more
quickly.

"Are you all right?" Des muttered, kissing his way
down her neck to her breast, leaving a wide trail of
fire.

She nodded, unsure of her ability to speak.

His thumb found her nipple and flicked it back and
forth. She hadn't know it could be the center of so
much pleasure, but wondrous sensations radiated out-
ward until there was no part of her left unaffected.
Even her fingertips were singed.

Another moan escaped her, then another, as his
mouth closed over the rigid tip and began to suck.
Her fingers slid through his hair and pressed his head
harder against her.

Over the years she had awakened with the memory
of the dreams she had had in the night. They had been
filled with a boy, a man, but she had never been able
to tell who he was. Now she knew her dreams had
been of Des. He was here, kissing her and touching
her and driving her out of her mind. Her dreams had
come to life.

"I want you."

Had she said it or had he?

"I want you," he said again.

A statement or a warning? Either way, it didn't
matter. His voice was deeper and rougher than she
had ever heard it, another sign that she was affecting
him every bit as much as he was affecting her.

"Say you want me, too." His words came out on a hot breath that fanned over her breast.

"I want you."

With a groan, he lifted his head and returned to her lips. Draining, possessive kisses followed. Deep, endless kisses.

He shifted so that more of his body was against her, and even through the layers of their clothes, she could feel how hard he was, and his body heat was positively scorching her.

She was almost overwhelmed. She had spent years fighting against her feelings for him, but no more. She wanted him inside her now, yet at the same time she knew she wanted this lovemaking to last forever. She wanted everything, and she was going to do her best to get it.

Gently she pushed against him until she had some maneuvering room. She wasn't sure what to say to him, but she knew what to do.

Her trembling hand went to the button of his jeans and undid it, then the zipper. With equally trembling hands, he began to help. Time slowed. Their surroundings receded; their circumstances were forgotten. Jeans, boots, sweaters, panties, briefs—they all came off. Then heated skin rubbed against heated skin. His hardened sex throbbed against her tummy. Her swollen breasts pressed against his chest, her nipples nestled into the curling dark hair. It was almost too much, yet deep down she knew it wasn't enough.

She was so glad she hadn't known how astonishing making love to him was going to be, she thought hazily. Because if she had, she never would have been able to stay away from him for so long.

He had said that he wished he could paint her on that long ago day. If she could somehow paint him, the canvas would portray strength and intensity. If she could paint what she was feeling now, it would be a canvas of bright, vivid colors swirled in a fury of passion.

She pulled him down on top of her, gladly accepting his weight. He positioned himself between her legs, then pulled back his hips and entered her with one smooth stroke. She gasped, and then, as if she had done it a million times before, arched up to meet his next thrust. She desperately needed him to fill her completely, to possess her absolutely.

As he moved in and out of her, she clung to him, rubbing her hands over his back and buttocks, delighting in the feel of his muscles shifting and rolling beneath the sleek, satinlike texture of his skin. She was consumed by the hunger she felt for him. Desire burned so hotly in her, she felt sure she would burst into flames at any moment.

It was as she had known all along— Des was a dangerous man to her.

She clutched at him, her fingers digging into his shoulders. "Des."

Des heard her whisper his name, heard the need and raw desire in her tone, and it was all the encouragement he needed. He pulled back his hips and drove as deeply as he could possibly manage into her tight velvet depths. Time and again he repeated the action,

pounding into her until sweat sheened his body and
his heart threatened to beat out of his chest. Caught
up in the feral, heated rhythm, he was helpless to do
anything else. Someone would have had to put a bul-
let in his head to stop him.

It was madness; it was ecstasy. He called her name
over and over. Then heaven shuddered through him,
followed by a thunderous, savage pleasure, and the
world spun away, leaving only the two of them, cling-
ing tightly to one another.

She loved Des.

Kit closed her eyes as the truth hit her with the
force of a Texas tornado, stirring up a thousand
thoughts and fears.

What was she going to do?

It was a beautiful, clear, cold day. The sun glinted
off the pristine layer of snow that had fallen during
the night, but the day's beauty barely registered with
her. Des filled her thoughts. And his silence pounded
against her ears as he guided his truck along the icy
track toward NW Section 158.

In fact, he had said very little since they had left
the cabin, but he didn't have to speak. As he had with
her, she knew what was going on with him.

Earlier, before she had come fully awake, she had
felt him enter her, and when the ultimate ecstasy
had come, it had been even greater than what they
had shared in the night.

Even amidst the passion, she had been aware that

it was much more than sex for her. But unfortunately, with the same sure feeling, she had also known it had been nothing more than sex to Des.

Now, in the bright light of day, Des no doubt was worried.

For years he had successfully navigated the minefields she and her sisters had attempted to lay for him. Then, during one snow-filled night, his resistance had crumbled.

But it wasn't his fault. Passion had flared in circumstances guaranteed to tempt even an angel, and he had given in to it. Now, though, he must be feeling monumental regret and wondering how he was going to back out of the trap he probably felt closing around him.

Besides the fact that it would be incredibly embarrassing to watch him try to gracefully maneuver back out of her life, she loved him too much to watch him try. She had to do something to help him. Later she would try to figure out how to help herself.

"You know, last night really meant nothing," she said in an attempt to reassure him, then inwardly flinched. She had spoken without thinking through what she was going to say and had phrased it very badly.

"Is that right?"

There was a touch of sarcasm in his tone that alerted her to the fact that he wasn't in the best of moods. She couldn't blame him.

She knew that another woman might see the night they had spent together as license to start making demands on him, perhaps even to plan a future for the two of them. But he had nothing to fear from her. If nothing else, she was a realist. She understood all too well that what had happened was a one-time-only event, a night of ecstasy she would remember the rest of her life, but a night never to be repeated.

As for Des, he was a man, and men were experts at compartmentalizing their lives and forgetting things that were too inconvenient to remember.

"It's just that I don't want you to worry that I'll read more into what happened last night than was really there."

"And I'm supposed to thank you for that?" His eyes glinted with dark anger.

She bent her head and gazed down at her tightly entwined fingers. "I'm sorry, Des."

"For *what?*"

"For a lot of things. For making you feel, however unintentionally, that you should help me find out who really killed Cody. But most of all I'm sorry for not listening to you when you said the weather was going to get worse."

He gave an impatient wave of his hand. "Don't worry about it."

"But I do. I—"

"Forget it. No one can predict Texas weather with any degree of accuracy. Not even professional weathermen. What makes you think you should have done it better?"

"You knew."

"It was an informed guess."

"And one I should have made, but I was too caught up in my problems."

"It's understandable."

"Still—"

"You *don't* owe me anything, Kit, much less an apology. There they are now." He pointed toward two men, who had stopped working on the fence and were watching them approach. He pulled the truck to a stop. "Are you okay about talking to them?"

"Of course."

"Then just signal me if you need any help."

"Okay." She hesitated, hating his abruptness. The knowledge that she loved him was so new it was throwing her. But she needed to regain her balance fast. Somehow she was going to have to find a way to deal with the fact that she loved him, and she was going to have to do it alone. But his continued bad mood bothered her, so much so that she tried again to reach out to him. "Des, maybe we should talk about it."

"You mean about what happened last night?"

He had known exactly what she was talking about—proof it was on his mind too. "Yes."

He gestured curtly. "It happened. It was great. There's nothing to talk about."

For a moment, she sat perfectly still, absorbing his brusque dismissal and searching for something to say that would ease the tension between them. She failed.

Then, because there was nothing else she could do, she climbed out of the truck and went to greet the two men who had worked on the ranch ever since she could remember. "Good morning, guys."

Burt greeted them with a wave. "Mornin', Kit, Des." He was tall and as thin as the toothpick that perpetually protruded from one corner of his mouth.

"Sure is nice to see you two," Red said, a grin plastered on his weathered face. He had been named after the color of his hair, though with age it had turned the shade of sand.

"You too. Did you all decide to camp out last night?"

Burt spat tobacco toward the fence post. "It was easier than fighting our way back in the storm."

"Figured we could have gotten lost if we weren't careful," Red added.

"But were you able to stay warm okay?"

"Shoot, yeah." Red pointed toward the roll tied at the back of his saddle. "We had all the comforts of home."

Burt repositioned his hat. "Fact is, I'd rather sleep outside. Don't cotton much to being cooped up. Never have."

Des smiled. "I never expected you to say anything else. Still, it's good to hear you made it through the night without getting cold."

Kit stuck her hands in the pockets of her jeans. "I agree." She had a sudden thought. If the men had returned to the cabin last night, she and Des wouldn't have made love.

If that hadn't happened, would she ever have admitted to herself that she loved him? Or would she have continued to go blindly through life without acknowledging how she felt? And in the end, which way would have been better?

Ultimately, though, it didn't matter. From now on, her life was going to be more difficult, but the fact remained that she would be forever grateful that she had had last night with Des.

"Listen, guys, I have a couple of things I'd like to ask you. It's about Cody Inman."

Red shook his head. "Heard about what happened."

Burt spat again. "Quite a shocker to know someone who got murdered."

"Right," Red said. "First time that ever happened."

Burt made a sound of agreement. "First time."

"That's the way we feel, too," Des said.

Kit shifted, trying to bank down her impatience with the men's chatty ways. "Does either of you know of anyone who might have fought with him or even wanted him dead?"

Red whistled. "Well, now, Kit, that's quite a question."

"You see, we really didn't know him all that well," Burt added.

Kit quietly sighed. She probably should have phrased the question more tactfully, but besides the murder, she now had Des and her love for him on her mind, and being diplomatic seemed beyond her. "Let me put it this way. Does either of you know anything about him that might help us figure out who killed him?''

Both men stared at her. With Burt and Red, one needed to pass the time of day for a while before getting to the real point. But time wasn't on her side.

''Anything at all?'' Des asked.

Red shrugged.

Burt looked at Kit. ''Rumor is you had some trouble with him.''

''That's right.''

Red nodded. ''He had a reputation with the ladies, that one did.''

Des's eyes narrowed. ''What do you mean?''

''He was somethin' of what you might call— excuse me for sayin' this in front of you, Kit— a womanizer.''

''There was sure that,'' Red said. ''From all accounts he was a real piece of work with women. Must have seen the main chance with you, Kit.''

''I suppose so.'' She just wished she had realized that truth sooner. ''Do you have any details that might back that up for us?'' *Us.* There was that word again. It was going to be a hard habit to break.

Burt shook his head. ''Not really.''

''Not exactly dates and times,'' Red said. ''But I did hear there was a married woman in El Paso who was on the verge of divorcing her husband for Inman. But Inman, he wasn't exactly what you'd call the marryin' kind, so he hightailed it out of town.''

Burt grinned. ''With her husband chasin' him every step of the way.''

Kit glanced up at Des, wondering if he was thinking the same thing as she. This was the first she had heard about Cody and other women. Was it possible he had been killed over one? And, if so, who?

"I suppose it was just a matter of time before someone took a tire iron to the son of a bitch," Red added.

"Tire iron?" Des fired out the question before she could. "You think he was killed with a tire iron?"

Red suddenly appeared uncomfortable. "Well, now, I can't really say. I was just talkin', you understand."

"Sure." Kit smiled, hoping it would soothe away some of his discomfort. "Thanks for your help, guys."

Once again Burt spat. "Don't seem like we did too much."

Red's forehead grooved with concern. "Hey, you're not in any real trouble, are you, Kit?"

She hesitated. "No, of course not."

"'Cause if you want us to do somethin' about that sheriff, we'd be mighty pleased to help out."

They were a throwback to another time, she realized with affection. However bad the idea was, she was touched at their offer to help. The truth was, she was rapidly becoming convinced that being in love with Des was going to give her far more trouble than the sheriff ever could. "I appreciate that, guys. Really I do. But I'm going to be okay."

"Okay, well, good, then." Burt spat.

* * *

The trip back to the homestead seemed to take twice as long as the trip out had taken, Des reflected darkly. But it was probably just him. From the start of the trip, Kit had been excruciatingly polite to him. Damn it, she had even apologized for saying she had wanted to stay at the cabin to wait for Burt and Red.

That had turned out to be the best part of the whole trip, which made it obvious as hell what she really wanted to apologize for was the fact that they had made love. That message was so clear, she might as well have yelled it at him.

Her attitude galled him. Where in the hell did she get off thinking there was any need to apologize? *He* had been the one who had started everything by telling her about his winter memories of her. And as he had, he had looked over at her and realized how much he wanted her. It had been just that simple, just that complicated. After that, it would have been impossible to keep his hands off her. And he had no intention of apologizing for that or for anything else.

He had also been the one who had started that kiss when she had been seventeen. His hands tightened on the steering wheel as he remembered that summer evening. She had looked so beautiful, with tears darkening her vivid green eyes and pieces of hay stuck in her tumbled red hair. His aching for her had hit bone, but he'd had to slam on the brakes. She had been only seventeen—way too young, way too innocent.

But last night had been different, and he had seen no reason to stop. She was older now, more experienced, and, if possible, even more beautiful. Plus, she had been completely willing.

In his mind, two consenting adults equaled a night of passion. However, always before he had known exactly what would happen the next morning. If he didn't want to see the woman again, he would simply bid her goodbye and make sure she got home safely. If he made the decision to see her a few more times, he would send her a bouquet of flowers, then follow them up with a phone call.

But in this case he had no idea what to do. Kit got to him like no other woman ever had before. And last night had been more than just another winter memory for his mental scrapbook. Last night had been branded into his flesh.

She was so damned independent, so damned wild. For all he knew, her apology meant she was trying to politely close the door against any further personal relationship between the two of them. But if that was the case, he was somehow going to have to change her mind.

When he had come home, he had initially intended to find out why she had started to avoid him since her sisters had married. He still didn't have that answer, but now it didn't seem to matter quite as much. Things had changed. The present circumstances had given him more than enough reason to be alone with her. For the time being, he planned to use those circumstances to his advantage.

Once Inman's murder was solved and no longer hanging over her head, that reason would be taken away. By then he hoped he wouldn't have to invent other reasons to be with her. But if he had to, he definitely would. Now that he'd had her, it was going to be impossible for him to get enough, at least as long as this clawing need for her lasted.

Seven

Des stopped his truck in front of Kit's house and nodded toward the familiar van. "Looks like Ada de la Garza is here again."

"Someone must have let her into the house." Kit stared at her front door. "A dictionary could use the woman's picture to define the words *rude* and *aggressive.*"

"Just remember, you're under no obligation to tell her a thing, so don't let her hound you into it."

Kit smoothed her hair back from her face and reached for the door handle. "I understand that, but it looks as if the stigma of this murder is sticking to me whether it's deserved or not, so I should at least make an attempt to tell her my side of the story. Otherwise, who knows what she'll write?"

"Don't be stupid, Kit. She just wants the opportunity to put quotes around a few of your phrases. But I'll guarantee she'll take those phrases out of context and make you look as guilty as hell."

"Stupid?" She climbed down from the truck, but Des was there before she had taken two steps toward the house.

"Is stupid the only word you heard me say? Because, if so, let me rephrase it. *Don't* talk to that woman."

"I can handle this myself, Des." She couldn't believe she was once again arguing with him about basically the same thing as before. Now *there* was something that could rightfully be construed as stupid. But she didn't want to argue with him anymore. In fact, not ever again. With their lovemaking still so fresh in her mind, she just couldn't cope with it.

"Have you forgotten what happened the last time she was here? The things she accused you of?"

"No, I haven't. And that's exactly why I need to talk to her. Maybe I can sway her toward the truth, and if I can, even just a little, it's bound to help."

"Kit—"

"We're not going to argue about this, Des. Not again. Now please get out of my way."

Ada de la Garza wore the same camera-flattering red wool suit she had worn before, and this time, there *was* a camera. She had brought a photographer with her, and the man was currently walking around the living room, holding up a light meter.

"May I call you Ada?" Kit figured she might as well, since the woman called her Kit.

Ada smiled, revealing her perfectly capped teeth. "Of course you may. Now, Kit, tell me about your relationship with Cody, and please start from the beginning."

"That's just it, Ada. You need to understand that there was no relationship."

She glanced over at Des. He was leaning against the doorjamb, his moody gaze constantly moving from her to the reporter, to the photographer, then back to her again. And whenever he looked at her, she felt heat. She rubbed the skin of her forearm as if she could banish the feeling. It didn't work.

She remembered every detail of their lovemaking, and it seemed like only minutes since they'd been together at the cabin, wrapped tightly in each other's arms. It had been as if they were the only two people left on earth.

"But, Kit, you were with him the night before his murder. People *saw* you."

"That's true, but it was just a casual thing."

Ada shook her head. "No, that can't be right. People who saw you two together said it didn't look at all casual. In fact, they said it looked downright sizzling. You can do a lot with your money, Kit, but you can't rewrite history."

"If that's what you think I'm doing, then you're wrong."

Ada's left eyebrow rose in a dramatic peak. "I'm an excellent writer, but I'm at a loss to know exactly how to report this story so that my readers will believe what you're saying.''

''How about just writing the truth?''

''Which is?''

The woman was a certified bitch and definitely had it out for her. Still, she had to continue to try to get through to her. ''All we did was dance. Cody read much more than was there into the situation.''

''Really? My goodness, if all you did was dance, it doesn't make much sense that he would do that, does it?''

''No, it doesn't.''

For the first time since they had begun to talk, the woman wrote down something on her notepad. ''Then why do you think he would do that? I mean, if you didn't lead him on—''

''And I didn't.''

''But what about what other people saw?''

''They misinterpreted what they saw.''

''Gracious me,'' Ada said, writing something else. ''If I take what you're saying as gospel, it seems everyone is wrong about what happened that night but you.''

''Look, Ada, I'm afraid we've got a case here where the only other person who could tell you what really happened is dead. And even if he were alive, he might not tell you the truth. And I don't have much to say that won't cast Cody in a bad light. It's unfortunate, but that's the way it is.''

''If you don't mind my saying, you don't seem very sorry that he's dead.''

She minded a great deal, but she also knew it wasn't going to do any good. "Once again, you're wrong."

"And once again, you're the only one who's right. How fascinating." Her pen flew over the notebook as she wrote. "I guess it has to do with being so rich."

"No—"

A light flashed as the photographer clicked off a picture.

Kit flinched, and Ada's smile broadened. If it wouldn't add fuel to the woman's story, she would throw her out of the house, notebook and all.

"If you're not going to believe what I say, then why did you even bother to come out here?"

"Why, Kit, I'm surprised you have to ask. It's not my job to believe or disbelieve you. I'm completely neutral. As a reporter, it's my job to report both sides."

She rose. "Okay, then, you have the truth of what happened. Report it."

The photographer took another picture. Before Kit could react, Des had the photographer by his elbow and was ushering him out the door.

Ada gazed after the two men, her mouth momentarily agape. "Excuse me, but I *am* correct in believing this is *your* house, am I not? That should mean that Mr. Baron doesn't have the right to throw anyone out without your say."

Kit shrugged. "Oh, I don't know. He probably has as much right as the photographer had to take my picture."

"We're here for a story, Kit. What did you expect?"

"Professionalism."

"Mr. Baron's actions were very protective. Does that mean you're having an affair with him, too?"

"That's none of your business." She suddenly realized that a night without sleep had caught up to her and she was very tired.

"Right," Ada said, standing. "But Mr. Baron manhandled my photographer, and I'm pretty sure he hurt him."

"It's entirely possible. I suggest you go see about him. Oh, and don't forget to write about what happened, either."

"Believe me, my story will be a doozy." The woman left with a beaming smile.

Kit groaned and fell back onto the sofa.

"They're gone," Des said as he returned and sat down beside her.

"I hate to say this, but no matter how objectionable they were, throwing that guy out was a mistake."

Des shrugged. "So let him sue me."

"He may just do that."

"He'll lose." His voice was both confident and deadly.

She sighed. "This is my fault."

"There you go again, taking everything on yourself."

A day ago she might have snapped his head off, but a day ago she hadn't known the glory of his lovemaking. ''Cody was a real jerk, and I didn't see it. Why?''

He slid his hand beneath her hair to her neck. ''Lighten up on yourself. From what Burt and Red said, the guy was a charmer.''

''Which I should have been able to recognize as false.'' Except that she had been too busy trying to avoid Des.

''Yeah, you probably should have.''

''Thanks.''

''You're the one who said it. I was only agreeing.''

She sighed. ''I know, but the fact that you're right doesn't make it any easier to hear.''

''I understand. But now that the subject is out in the open…''

''Which subject?'' His hand on her skin had begun to work its magic. When it came to him, her body was incredibly compliant.

''I asked you this once before, but you never really gave me an answer. Why did you go out with him in the first place?''

She shifted, changing her position so that his hand dropped away. ''As I recall, I did answer you.''

''No, actually we got sidetracked.''

She believed him. They could become sidetracked with the greatest of ease. ''Cody was just an opportunity to go dancing.''

''And that was important to you? So important you'd go with just anyone?''

''He wasn't just anyone. He had always been very pleasant. He was a good dancer and good company.

Don't make this into the mystery of the century, Des. I went with him, and we had a good time until... Well, you know what happened."

"It just doesn't seem like something you'd do, that's all."

"How would you know what I would or wouldn't do? You don't know me. Not really." Actually, she was wrong, she reflected ruefully. In some ways he knew her better than was good for her peace of mind. He knew just where to touch her to make her come undone, just where to kiss her to make her forget everything....

But he didn't know she loved him yet, and she had to take care that he never did.

"I'm not being critical, Kit." He paused. "Well, maybe indirectly I am, but I don't mean to be. It's just that when it comes to the Double B and everything concerned with it, you're very conscientious. Always have been. And the night you went into town with Cody wasn't a weekend. Both of you had to work the next day."

"What can I say? You're right."

"Then why?"

She exhaled a long breath. "Haven't we gone over this?"

"In part, but it still bothers me."

"Look, I shouldn't have gone, but..." She couldn't tell him that she had gone in a knee-jerk reaction to his arrival, so she told him another truth. "My father made it a point never to socialize with anyone who worked for him. I think he felt it would undermine his position of authority if he let his guard down even once.''

''Now that you mention it, I don't think I ever saw him at any of the ranch's social occasions that involved the hands.''

''No, you didn't. In fact, he felt all social occasions were frivolous. He only tolerated them if they involved business and he knew he could gain something by attending.''

''Now I remember my dad saying something about that. Your father had a very narrow point of view about life, Kit. He should be pitied.''

''Pitied? What a remarkable and preposterous idea.''

His hand reached out to touch her again, and his thumb grazed up and down the side of her neck. He smiled. ''Okay, so that was a stretch. But did you just hear yourself? You basically said that you went out with Cody because your father never went out with people who worked for him.''

She had to wrench her gaze from his lips. ''I may have said that. It may even have been an underlying reason. But the main reason I like to socialize with Double B people is that I *like* them.'' It was another very real truth.

''And they like and respect you. But—''

''But the bottom line is that, in this case, I was a poor judge of character.''

''No, the bottom line is that there is no simple truth.'' He paused. ''You know, I never realized just how much your father has to answer for.''

"My father's been gone a long time, Des. The truth is, I should have known better. If I'd stopped to think for even *one* minute…" She rubbed her forehead.

"It's not your fault. Something must have happened. Maybe something about work was getting you down."

Now he was defending her. "No."

"Then what?"

"Let's just forget about it. There's no point in going over and over this." She pushed herself up from the sofa and began to pace. "I went out with Cody and now he's dead. The sheriff thinks I killed him, and so do a lot of other people. And you and I haven't found anything to prove otherwise."

He reached out and pulled her down on his lap. "But we will, Kit. We will."

Suddenly his arms were around her, and she felt totally engulfed by him. "How can you be so sure?"

"I just am."

She gave a nervous half-laugh. "Oh, a jury is going to buy that one for sure."

Another smile tugged at his lips. "I can be very convincing when I set out to be."

He was preaching to the choir. She was already a believer. "But if even one of them doesn't agree—"

"It's not going to happen. As a matter of fact, there's not even going to be a trial."

"But that first night you said—"

"I was just trying to anticipate what might happen. I was wrong."

"The great Des Baron wrong? That's hard for me to believe."

"It happens very seldom."

He was trying to make her laugh, and she appreciated his efforts, but she was frightened, and she didn't know how to handle the fear. Even more, she was in love and, because of it, off balance. It made thinking hard.

"Maybe my father was right in his belief that it was wrong to socialize with the people who work for you."

"He was wrong and you know it." His hand slid up to the side of her face and turned her so that she had no choice but to look at him. "I want to tell you something, and I want you to believe what I'm saying. In every way I can think of, you're far more successful than your father ever thought of being. Unfortunately, you're also incredibly vulnerable."

His words stunned her, and she didn't know how to reply.

"Looking back, I should have tried to get closer to you when you were growing up. Maybe I could have helped in some way."

"There's no reason for you to feel that I way. I did okay. Tess, Jill and I *all* did okay, and I don't know why you're bringing it up now." She needed to get away from him.

"I'm not really sure. Maybe because of what I said yesterday. That you were wonderful back then and you are wonderful now, and there's no reason for you to apologize for anything to anyone."

"Fine. I won't." She pushed against him, but his arm tightened around her.

"Don't go. Stay."

His arms were strong around her, and it would have been so easy to let herself relax into him. But unrequited love only brought pain. Why compound that pain? With superhuman effort, she broke free of his hold and slid off his lap to her feet.

"What's wrong, Kit?"

"Nothing."

He surged to his feet. "Then why are you trying to run away from me?"

"That's not what I'm doing at all. It's just that I don't think we should let ourselves get carried away. You said it yourself. Last night happened. It was great. There's nothing left to talk about."

"I was wrong when I said that. It wasn't just great, it was sensational."

She took a step backward. "There's a lot going on right now. Emotions are running high, and not just ours, either. But we need to remember that I'm suspected of murder and you're my lawyer."

"So far I agree with you," he said, his voice wooden.

"Good, because when you think about it, the stakes are enormous. It would be far better to keep our relationship on a purely business level."

"That's where I disagree."

"Then you're not thinking with your *brain.*"

A muscle flexed along his jaw. "Once again, I agree with you."

As much as she ached for him, she couldn't let this dissolve into another night of lovemaking. Because if she did, somewhere in the midst of it, in some way, she would slip up and he would realize she loved him. If that happened, he would exit her life so fast, her head would spin.

And she wasn't only thinking of protecting *him* now. Pride she hadn't been aware of had come rushing into play. How could she ever face him if he knew she loved him? She couldn't.

Basically it had come down to the fact that she had to rescue herself.

"Last night was nothing more than a one-night stand, Des."

"And we were doing so well there." Beneath his mock regret, she heard a caustic tone so corrosive, she could feel it eating at her.

"It's true."

He reached out for her, but she managed to slip out of his way.

"Des, *listen* to me. I don't *want* to spend the night with you again."

His sudden stillness sent a chill through her. His eyes darkened until all light had vanished into black.

"I guess, when you put it like that, I can't argue with you."

Eight

"**G**ood morning."

Kit nearly knocked over her coffee cup as Des strolled into her office the next day, wearing tight jeans and a leather vest over a navy blue flannel shirt. His inherent power and raw sexuality suddenly made her uncomfortably aware of everything that was feminine in her. One way or another, he was her undoing.

"What are you doing here?"

His lips quirked. "You need to work on your hospitality, Kit."

"You know what I mean. After last night, I didn't expect to see you—not so soon, anyway." She knew she was saying everything wrong, but at this point she had no clue how to stop. Perhaps she should simply say nothing.

"Did you really expect me to slink off and hide under a mesquite somewhere like a wounded animal?"

Saying nothing was not going to work. His anger was well earned, and he deserved a response. "No, of course not. It's just that when you left you seemed...upset."

"Angry, maybe. Confused definitely. Conflicting signals sometimes do that to me."

What could she say to that? This time she took her own advice and said nothing, which was apparently fine with him. He headed to the sideboard, where he poured himself a cup of coffee, leaving her time to try to regain her composure. Except it was extremely difficult.

She loved him and had shared a night of passion with him that she would never forget and never regret. But she had also done something else. She had made a decision to let him off the hook about their shared night together and, while she was at it, had safeguarded her pride and her heart. She had told him that what had happened had meant nothing, when in fact it had meant everything.

In retrospect, she had been neither logical nor rational when she had told him that. Then again, logical and rational were two words rarely associated with love.

"Why are you here, Des?"

Taking his time, he seated himself in front of her desk, crossed his long legs and took several sips of coffee. Then he gazed around the office, uncrossed his legs, eyed his coffee with interest and crossed his legs one more time. Just as her nerves were about to snap, he looked at her.

"Did you sleep well last night?"

"*That's* why you're here? To ask me that?"

"Did you?"

"Yes, I did." It was the truth. Despite the turbulent state of her emotions, she had managed to fall into a deep sleep. But she had dreamed. Oh, had she dreamed.

"I didn't."

"That's too bad." It was an automatic, courteous thing to say, but she couldn't come up with anything else.

"Don't you want to know why?"

"No." In his present mood, there was no telling what he would say. "*Why* are you here?"

"To see you." He paused, his intense dark gaze igniting warmth along her nerve endings. "No comeback, Kit?"

"No."

"That's a shame. I would have been extremely interested in what you could come up with."

"Disappointments are part of life."

"There now. That's a nice comeback. Congratulations."

"Des?"

"Yes, Kit?"

She drew a steadying breath. He was putting her through hell, and who was to say she didn't deserve it? Not her.

He held up a pacifying hand. "I'm also here because Bill Ridley called me early this morning."

"He called you?"

"I believe that's what I said."

If it had been anyone else who had addressed her in that cool, arrogant way, she would have verbally cut them down to size, then thrown them out. But it wasn't just anyone else. It was Des.

"It's just that Bill called me, too."

"Then you know that Scooter Garner and Johnny Don Galvez are back from Oklahoma City."

Now he was being all business, but she was as disconcerted as she had been before. "As a matter of fact, I asked Bill to send them over." She glanced at her watch. "I'm expecting them any minute."

"Then I'll wait."

"You don't have to."

"Yes, I do. Remember? I'm getting to see you. Plus, we've got a little matter of murder going on here, and I'm your lawyer. I know you haven't forgotten that, because you told me so just last night."

He smiled in the same way she had once seen a tiger smile on a *National Geographic* special. The tiger had smiled like that right before he pounced on his prey.

"Are those enough reasons, or do you want more?" he asked. "Because if you do, I'm sure I could—"

"Ms. Baron?"

Kit visibly jumped. She had been so wrapped up in Des and the tiger image that she hadn't even heard the two men arrive. "Scooter, Johnny Don—please come in and sit down."

Both men looked ill at ease, but nevertheless, they swept off their hats and chose chairs. They were in their late twenties and seasoned cowboys. Their browned skin attested to long hours spent in the sun, and their solid muscles spoke of the hard physical work they did every day.

"You both know Mr. Baron, right?" she asked, trying to put them at ease.

"Sure thing," Scooter said. "Morning, Mr. Baron."

Johnny Don nodded. "Morning."

"Please call me Des."

Kit pointed toward the sideboard. "Would either of you like some coffee?"

"No, thank you."

"No, thank you."

She inwardly sighed. She guessed she just needed to jump right into the subject. "Okay, then, the reason I asked you to come in this morning is because I'd like to ask you a few questions about Cody Inman."

"Shame about what happened to him," Scooter said.

"Damn shame," Johnny Don said.

All the men she had talked to had said pretty much the same thing, so she wasn't surprised to hear it from them. Plus, a murder where you worked would make anyone nervous.

"It *is* a shame, and I'm trying to help figure out who might have killed him."

Des cleared his throat.

"*We* are," she amended, with a glance at him.

Scooter shook his head. "I didn't see a thing."

"Me either," Johnny Don said, looking slightly alarmed.

"We didn't think you did, but we heard you were both at the same poker game as Cody was the night before he was murdered."

"That's right."

"Uh-huh."

"Did you see or hear anything that night that could help us find out who might have killed Cody?"

Scooter shook his head. "It was just a regular poker game."

Johnny Don tapped his hat against his knee. "It was already going by the time he got there. Nothing much was said except about what was happening with the game."

"By any chance did he win?" Des asked.

Scooter glanced around at him. "Not that I can remember."

"He didn't win," Johnny Don said with assurance. "Not a thing."

"Did that make him mad?"

"Naw." Scooter grinned. "When you play poker, you win sometimes and you lose sometimes. Everyone knows that. And if you don't, you don't belong in the game."

She felt as if she were pounding her head against a brick wall. In fact, it might feel better than this.

"Do you know anyone, anyone at all, who might have wanted him dead?"

Surprisingly, neither of them answered right away.

Scooter looked over at Johnny Don, then back at her. "I guess he had his faults, but then, I don't know any angels."

"None of us do," Des murmured. "But unfortunately, Cody's murder has thrown the spotlight on him, and we're having to look for a reason why someone was so angry with him that they killed him."

Scooter shrugged. "Putting it that way, I suppose there could have been a few."

"Women, mainly," Johnny Don said. "He had a way of getting women to fall for him, then leaving them."

There it was again, the suggestion that a woman somehow could have been involved in the murder, and it was completely plausible. There were plenty of women who worked on the Double B, or who were wives and daughters of men who did. And from what Burt and Red had said, she couldn't rule out married women, either.

She edged up in her chair. "Is there some specific situation you're referring to?" she asked.

"Not really. Actually, none of us were too happy with Cody that night."

"Why's that?" Des asked.

In the other interviews he had let her do most of the questioning, but now he must feel, as she did, that they were getting close to the truth.

Johnny Don gazed at his hat as if it was the most

fascinating thing he had ever seen. "He was doin' some bragging."

"About being out with me, you mean?"

"Uh-huh."

He had just confirmed what she had previously suspected. The first person she had interviewed, Scott McKee, had told them that Cody had mentioned he had been out with her, and she had guessed Cody had probably bragged about it.

"Fact of the matter is," Scooter said, "no one at that game was real happy with Cody. It was a work night, and there he was, getting drunk and shooting off his mouth. It wasn't right."

"Mike wasn't happy with him, either."

"Mike? Mike Stillwell?"

"Mike Stillwell," Johnny Don confirmed.

Without realizing what she was doing, she looked at Des. "He's the one who's at his sister's funeral, isn't he?"

Des nodded at her. "That's right."

Johnny Don gazed at Des. "I never heard Mike say much about his sister before, but he was sure upset when he took off for the funeral."

"I think they were close," Scooter said. "He once told me he had raised her. Seems like I recall her name was Angie. I remember thinking it was a nice name."

"Then his parents must be dead?"

"Yep."

Kit hoped there was nothing in her manner that was giving away how tense she felt. If such a thing were truly possible, she was certain she would jump right out of her skin. "Is there anything else you can tell us about Cody?"

Johnny Don shook his head.

"Can't think of a thing," Scooter said.

Des stood and extended his hand, and both men followed suit. "Thank you for your time. We really appreciate you coming. And if you think of anything else that might be relevant, please call either Ms. Baron or me."

"Will do."

"Sure thing."

The men left to go back to work, and Des turned to her. "What do you think?"

"It's got something to do with a woman."

"I agree. Unfortunately, we still don't know whether that means a woman killed him, or whether he was killed over a woman."

"But jealousy seems a likely motive."

"Maybe."

She frowned. "Is there something I'm not getting?"

"No. It's just that I've been involved in a lot of murder cases, and if there's one thing I've learned, it's to not be surprised when something that seems clear turns out to be muddy as hell."

"Well, for now, everything looks clear. We've talked to everyone who was at that poker game except Mike Stillwell, and I think we need to talk to him next." She heard the *we* and changed it. "*I* need to talk to him."

A slight smile graced his mouth, though he didn't comment on her change of *we* to *I*. "You know, Kit, the murderer might not even have been at that poker game."

She stood. "Quit raining on my parade, Des. I'm going to follow the clues until I run out of them."

"And you're doing the right thing—the *only* thing you can do at this point. I just don't want you to be disappointed if you run into a dead end, that's all."

"Don't worry about it." She quietly sighed. She would give anything if the atmosphere between them weren't as strained as it was. But she accepted the full blame. It would be so much easier if she didn't love him....

"Kit—" His head swung toward the door. "Someone else is coming. Who are you expecting?"

"No one."

Sheriff Moreno walked in, the men close behind. "Sorry to interrupt your, uh—" his eyes narrowed on Des "—business meeting, Ms. Baron, but I brought some men to search your house."

"You *what?*"

Des surged to his feet. "You can't do that."

"Ah, yes, I can." With a smirk, he flourished a legal-looking document. "See for yourself."

Des took it from him, snapped it open and read. "He's got a search warrant, Kit."

Kit felt the room begin to tilt around her, and she quickly sat. "There must be some mistake. The homestead has *never* been searched." To her it was inconceivable. In her mind, the homestead had always been and would always be inviolate.

"There's no mistake." His gaze held steady on the sheriff. "What are you looking for?"

"Anything that can help us find out who killed Cody Inman. In addition, we still haven't found the murder weapon. And since Ms. Baron hasn't come in yet to be fingerprinted, I decided to keep the investigation moving forward in this way."

"What's your plan?"

"I've borrowed men from a couple of counties so we can search all the homestead buildings and the barns at the same time." He walked out into the hall and called, *"Get started."*

Kit watched in horror as strangers spread out through her house. The rest of the cars took off toward the barns.

"Just a minute, Moreno," Des said. "I want your promise that your people will be careful in the search."

"The men I brought today are the best."

"That's not the issue. I've seen well-trained men destroy a place, and I'm telling you now, they better handle everything they touch with kid gloves."

"I'm sure they will." His smile was entirely unpleasant. "In the meantime, you and Ms. Baron wait here while the process is being carried out."

"We'll wait. Just remember what I said."

The sheriff didn't even pretend to smile this time.

"Not even you, Baron, are powerful enough to get in the way of justice."

"There's justice, and then there is justice."

"You're a high-priced lawyer, Baron, and I know you could stand there and argue with me all day long and never cover the same subject twice. So there's no way I'm going to waste my time arguing with you. Stay here with Ms. Baron, and I'll be back in a few minutes."

Des stared after the sheriff, fighting the urge to go after him. He would gain an immeasurable amount of personal satisfaction if he could just beat the hell out of the man. But in the end, he knew he would accomplish nothing.

He turned back into the room. Kit had lost all color in her face. Lord, he needed to help her, and he didn't know how. There had been very few times in his life when he had felt as frustrated and as helpless as he did at this moment. But now all he could really do was wait with Kit.

She might not realize it, but he knew exactly how much this house meant to her. She had worked hard to make it into a home she could call her own. She had opened it up, allowed light into it, and decorated it with impeccable taste. She had personalized it in the most basic way and in the process wiped out all memories of her father from it.

Damn the sheriff.

While he had been with Kit at the cabin, the man had been working on the search warrant. Normally he thought several steps ahead of his opponent, but he had been so wrapped up in his need for Kit that he hadn't seen this coming.

Now what was he going to do?

"It'll be all right, Kit. They know that if they damage anything, I'll sue them to hell and back."

She wrapped her arms around herself and numbly nodded. "I'm sure you're right."

He would rather she rant and rail at him than mutely accept what was happening in this quiet, almost fragile way. He thrust stiffened fingers through his hair. "This is all my fault. I'm sorry. I should have anticipated that Moreno would do this."

"It's not anyone's fault. You're not a psychic."

"No, but I'm a lawyer, and I know damn well how things work."

She shrugged. "It's okay." A loud thud sounded somewhere on the second floor and drew her gaze to the ceiling.

It was too much for him. He moved purposefully toward the door.

"Don't, Des." Her quiet, calm voice halted him. "Let them work. The sooner they do what they came to do, the sooner they'll leave."

Her composure was shattering his. "You need some hot coffee."

The truth was, he needed to do something, anything. He poured a cup, then liberally dosed it with brandy. When he turned to her, he found her watching him with a calm, green-eyed gaze.

"You're pale," he said, explaining away the brandy.

She took the steaming cup from him. "You could use some, too."

"You're right." He helped himself and had downed about a third of it when the sheriff returned. "Find anything yet?"

"No, but then, we're not through, either."

"If you haven't found the murder weapon by now, I doubt you will anytime soon. It could have been thrown in one of the stock ponds or buried underneath that new snow we had."

Moreno shrugged. "We'll find it. It may take a while, but you can be sure we'll find it."

Kit spoke up. "Would you like a cup of coffee, sheriff?"

Moreno's face creased with brief surprise. "No thanks."

Des thought quickly. Maybe it would slow the sheriff down if he appeared to cooperate. He gestured to one of the chairs in front of Kit's desk. "Sit down, sheriff, and I'll bring you up to speed on our investigation."

"*Your* investigation?"

"Sit. Please."

In an unnecessary move, Moreno shifted his gun out of the way, then sat down. "Look, Baron, you're an experienced litigator, but I doubt you know anything about proper investigative technique."

"I know something about it." With a glance at Kit to make sure she was still all right, he took the other chair.

"I doubt it. Common sense tells me that you're too busy to do any investigating. You hire it out."

"Common sense," Kit repeated softly. "Now there's an idea."

A glance at the sheriff assured Des that her ironic comment had gone over the man's head.

The sheriff leaned forward. "You're not experienced in investigations, and I want you to leave it to me, Baron. Too many people tramping around over the same ground can make a big mess."

Des nodded. "I see your point. Then why don't you tell us what you've found out so far?"

"I'm not ready to disclose that information just yet." Moreno looked at Kit. "I want you to come back to town with me this afternoon and be fingerprinted."

Des spoke before she could. "Then you've found *hard* evidence that points to Ms. Baron?"

"I've got enough."

"What you have is circumstantial, and you know it, and I don't want Ms. Baron subjected to fingerprinting until you have something concrete."

Moreno's eyes narrowed. "I could have you charged with obstructing justice."

"Try it."

A vein pounded in the sheriff's forehead. "If Ms. Baron doesn't get herself into town within the next few days to be fingerprinted, I'll have a warrant issued for her arrest."

"You know you can't do that."

"I can do anything I want."

"Only for a limited period of time, and we both know it. So let me just caution you that arresting Ms. Baron wouldn't be advisable."

"You don't *advise* me."

The two men glared at each other.

Kit cleared her throat. "I assure you, Sheriff Moreno, the last thing Mr. Baron and I want to do is obstruct justice. Since I did *not* kill Cody Inman, we are rooting for you to find the person who did. As for not coming in to be fingerprinted, that's my fault. Business obligations." She said the two words as if they explained everything. "As for my seeing the men in question, in the course of running the ranch and on any given day, I naturally talk with quite a few of my hands."

With a certain amount of resignation, the sheriff pulled out his notebook and flipped to a certain page. "Who have you talked to?"

"A few of the people who were at the poker game the night before Cody was killed."

"Who?"

"Scott McKee."

Moreno nodded. "I talked with him."

"Get anything?" Des asked innocently.

The sheriff ignored him.

She continued. "Red Tinsdall and Burt Salatore."

"I have their names, but I haven't been able to locate them. Some manager told me they were working in a southern section and gave me directions. Took me nearly half a day to get out there, and when I did, no one was there."

She hid a smile. He had been told to go in the exact opposite direction of where the men actually were. "Our hands are trained to go where the work is, and that can change hourly. They must have been needed elsewhere."

"Damn inefficient way to run a business if you ask me."

"We've managed to have some success."

Her mild reply drew a sharp glance from him. "I plan to find those men today."

"I'm sure you will. In fact, I don't know which of my managers you saw, but I'll have Bill Ridley talk to you. He can tell you exactly where the men are."

"Good." Her cooperation seemed to pacify him.

"Sheriff, no one wants this case wrapped up quicker than I do."

"I'm sure." He checked his notebook again. "What about the other three? I was told Mike Stillwell was attending a funeral, and the other two were in Oklahoma getting supplies? Let's see... Scooter Garner and Johnny Don Galvez."

"Scooter and Johnny Don are back now. Again, Bill Ridley can tell you where to find them."

Moreno stood. "Then as soon as my men are finished here in the house, I'll go find this Bill Ridley."

"Fine."

She rose and held out her hand. "I know you're doing your best, Sheriff, and I appreciate it."

He paused and looked down at Des. "I understand Ada de la Garza paid you a visit and that there was a bit of a problem with her photographer."

Des casually lifted his shoulders. "No problem that I can think of."

"Both Ada and the photographer said you roughed him up."

"I merely showed him the door."

"They both used the term *roughly*."

"I like the term *firmly* better."

"I don't have time to play word games with you, Baron." Moreno nodded to her. "I'll be getting back to you."

"I'll be here."

As soon as he walked out of the office, Kit sank into her chair and took a drink of her spiked coffee. It tasted so good, she had another.

Des began to applaud. "You were superb with him. You handled him much better than I would have."

"That's because your temper gets the best of you whenever he's around."

"You've seen me angry, but you've never seen me lose my temper. Neither has he."

If that was the case, she hoped she never did. "I figured I didn't have anything to lose by going along with him."

"You were right."

In this case, being right didn't make her feel any better. It also didn't help her.

"But you're *not* going in to be fingerprinted."

"Whatever you say."

He paused. "You have quite a talent there, managing to humor both me and the sheriff."

"Is it working?"

"I'll let you know."

She smiled. No matter what the circumstances were, she was becoming accustomed to having Des around all the time. When the person who actually committed the murder was found, that would end. How was she going to stand the pain? "I better call Bill Ridley."

He nodded. "That's just what I was going to suggest."

She picked up the phone and punched in the number. "Bill, this is Kit. I've sent the sheriff your way."

On the other end of the line, Bill cursed. "He's going to be wasting his time."

"Don't perjure yourself for me. Just answer the questions as best you can."

"Sure thing, but, you know, I don't have a very good memory these days. Old age, I reckon."

"I appreciate your loyalty, Bill, but the truth is, I don't have anything to hide."

"Shoot fire, I never thought you did. It's just that from what I hear, this man is a donkey's hind end."

She took another drink of her brandy and coffee. "I'd have to agree with you there, but I just want to get this whole thing over with. Listen, the main reason I called is to ask how long you think Mike Stillwell is going to be gone for his sister's funeral?"

"I don't know. In cases like a death in the immediate family, the time off is open-ended."

Even though Bill couldn't see her, she nodded out of habit. "That's what I thought. Do you know where the funeral is being held?"

"I know the name of the town, because I notified the business manager's office so that the ranch could send flowers." She heard a shuffling of papers. "Here it is." He read off the name.

"Thanks, Bill. And by the way, I wouldn't mind if you didn't tell the sheriff about this."

"I can handle the man. Don't you worry about a thing."

"Thanks again, Bill." Such good advice. Too bad she couldn't follow it.

Next she dialed the business office and requested the name and location of the funeral home. When she hung up from them, she looked at Des. "I don't think it would hurt anything if I got to Mike before the sheriff does."

"I agree. Let's go."

She automatically started to tell him that she could go by herself, but ultimately she was too much in love with him to deprive herself of spending even a little more time with him.

"I'll order the helicopter."

Nine

Des.

Kit fell back onto the hotel bed, still dressed in the forest green cashmere sweater and matching suede skirt she had worn for the trip.

She looked up at the ceiling. It had been a long day. By rights she should be tired, but she had never felt more awake, more wired. The blame, if you could call it that, was her close proximity to Des, who was in the adjoining room.

Earlier, she and Des had landed in Oklahoma, rented a car and driven straight to the funeral home. It had taken only a moment's inquiry to find that the funeral had already been held. But when Des had inquired about any next of kin information, the funeral director had refused to tell him, stating that fraudulent practices were all too common and easy against those still mourning for departed loved ones. They'd had no choice but to check into a hotel. It was a long way from the five-star hotels they were both used to, but it was clean and had everything they needed for one night.

A lock clicked on the door to the adjoining room, and she heard the door open. A moment of silence was followed by a knock.

Des.

Though they hadn't asked for adjoining rooms, the clerk who had checked them in had arranged them. She went to open the door.

"Would you like to go down for dinner? I saw a coffee shop off the lobby. They may have some chili or something. Or we could go somewhere else."

His light blue shirt was open at the collar, revealing the column of his brown throat, and the long sleeves had been rolled up his strong forearms. Kit turned away and returned to sit on the bed. "No, thanks. I'm not hungry, but you can go if you like."

Their night of reckless lovemaking had reduced them to excruciating politeness, she reflected dully. When she glanced at the door again, she saw that he had disappeared. She could only imagine how much he disliked her now that she had told him their night together had meant nothing. Though her intentions had been the best, she couldn't find it in her to like herself very much, either. Surely there was a kinder way she could have said the same thing.

She briefly closed her eyes against the pain that knifed through her heart. Even though she had been trying to protect both of them, she now had a sickening feeling that she had acted precipitously. He was so close....

He reappeared with a phone book. "I've looked up the name Stillwell and have found quite a few. Why don't we divide them up and start calling? Who knows? Maybe we'll get lucky and Mike will answer."

"Good idea." It would at least give them something to do. She pulled her room's phone book from the built-in nightstand, and flipped to the correct page.

"I'll take the first half," he said. "You take the last."

She nodded and began calling. It took a while to get through the names, since several of the people turned out to be quite chatty and insisted on giving her the history of their family tree. However, none of them were able to tell her anything about a Mike or Angie Stillwell.

Next door, she heard a receiver drop onto its cradle; then Des strolled into her room and settled onto the bed next to her. "No luck?"

"No luck."

"Me either, but I've had another idea."

He looked at her. "What?"

"We require our prospective employees to give references. Mike might have given his sister as one. If he did, it will list her address and phone number. If not, maybe one of the references will be able to tell us where we can find him.''

''Great idea.''

In the light from the nightstand lamp, his eyes gleamed, and she found herself caught up in them. ''I—I don't know why I didn't think of it before now. It was such an obvious thing for me to do.''

''I said it earlier. You've had a lot on your mind. Plus, you don't handle the personnel end of the business.''

So what was his excuse for not thinking of it?

''There's just one problem. The personnel office at the ranch closes at 6:00 p.m. If I was home, I could probably track down someone who works there, but as it is, I left home without any of my numbers.''

''Don't worry about it. We're settled in for the night now. You can give them a call in the morning.''

She nodded, wondering what else she could say to keep the conversation going. She had tried earlier to bring up what had happened in the cabin, and he had cut her off. She felt she owed him apologies on so many levels, but he wouldn't want to hear them. And she was positive he was still angry about her comment that their night together had meant nothing. No doubt he was used to making that decision.

Then she thought of something. ''Remember when you told me about the memories you had of me when I was a young girl?''

''That's not something I'd forget.''

''Okay, well, I have some of you.'' He looked so surprised she almost laughed. ''I remember when you were about sixteen or so. There was this wild horse that no one could get close to. But one afternoon you went out to that corral and spent hours with him, talking to him, gentling him. You were amazing with him."

"Just like you are with Dia."

She shrugged off the compliment. "You were very special with that horse."

"I was just doing what I had learned from some of the older guys."

"Maybe, but with this particular horse, no one was having any luck until you came along. By the time the afternoon was over, that horse was literally eating out of your hand. By the next day you were riding him."

"Where you at the corral?"

"Not at the corral, no, but I was nearby."

"In one of the barns?"

"Yes. I was up in the hay door."

His lips quirked. "I had no idea."

Her gaze fixed on his lips, then returned to his eyes. "There was no reason why you should notice me."

He grinned. "In retrospect, I don't know how I could *not* notice you. I must have been blind."

"Not at all. You forget, I wasn't even a teenager at that point. Plus, at that age, the difference in our ages seemed larger than it actually was."

"If I was sixteen, you must have been around eleven."

"Right." She hesitated. "I remember the girls, too."

"Girls?"

This time she did laugh at his surprised look. "Don't act so innocent. Let's see, there were Donna, Melissa and Jennifer, just to name three. Don't you remember them?"

"Now that you said their names I do."

"I remember Donna, in particular, because you brought her to a wiener roast that, amazingly enough, I happened to get to go to, thanks to your dad. Somehow he managed to talk my father into letting me and my sisters go, though I'll never know how he did it. I was thrilled, though."

"A wiener roast? I don't remember. Seems like I went to a lot of wiener roasts, along with hay rides, barn dances, that sort of thing."

The way his forehead creased whenever he was thinking fascinated her. The way the crinkles beside his eyes became more pronounced when he smiled enchanted her. In fact, at this moment she couldn't think of a thing she didn't enjoy about him. "I'm sure you did, but I didn't. Being able to go was a big, big deal for me, so I remember this one very well. You were with Donna. And that night, as I recall, I experienced jealousy for the first time."

He grinned. "*You* jealous? I just can't imagine that. You've always seemed so self-contained."

"Ah, but you see, Donna was something I could never imagine being at that time—*sophisticated.*"

He laughed. "Donna? No, honey, I don't think so. If I was sixteen, then she was sixteen."

Honey. Warmth flooded her, an outsized reaction

to an offhand remark. She was beyond hope. "Let me assure you that in comparison to me she was definitely sophisticated. And there was more. She was on an actual *date* with you. I couldn't even imagine such an exotic thing. And she seemed so comfortable with you."

He slid his hand up through her hair. "But you're comfortable with me now, right?"

She hadn't anticipated his move. She waited a moment until her equilibrium returned. It didn't. "Uh, no, not when you do things like you're doing now."

"What? Touching you? But we've spent the night together. You remember that, don't you?"

Did he seriously think she could forget? "Of course I do, but it doesn't mean that I'm, um, actually accustomed to having you touch me."

His fingers moved restlessly in her hair. "Why not? Didn't I do it enough?"

"Yes, but—"

His other hand found the rapidly beating pulse at the base of her neck. "I remember that I kissed this spot right here." He bent his head and pressed his mouth to the spot. "And then I remember kissing you right here." He kissed the same place behind her other ear.

She closed her eyes as warmth rivered through her. "This isn't fair."

"Who said it was?"

His lips smoothed up her throat and stopped at the sensitive area behind her ear.

"And then I distinctly remember touching you here."

His hand closed over her breast, and she smothered a moan.

"I also did this a lot," he said huskily as he caressed her breast, lightly massaging and rubbing her until she was fearful for her mind.

"Des…" The word *stop* stuck in her throat. Even though she knew all the reasons why she should say it, she couldn't. What he was doing felt too good for her to say anything.

"I also remember unhooking your bra and doing this."

Magically her bra was unhooked; then his palm lightly pushed against her rigid nipple and rolled it round and round until she had to reach out for him to stay upright.

"What are you doing?" she asked, gasping for breath.

He leaned his body weight into her and pressed her down to the bed. "Why don't you just consider this an extension of our one-night stand?"

There it was, proof that he was still angry with her. But he also still wanted her.

"Oh, Des…" She heard the surrender in her voice. If it were possible, she wanted him even more than she had wanted him that night.

She was his.

Whether he liked it or not. Whether she liked it or not.

They could be in the hayloft of a barn or a faraway cabin, even in an Oklahoma hotel room. Forever and always, she would be his.

Her inhibitions evaporated. Her clothes disappeared. One by one, she felt her bones melt. Then his fingers stroked up her thigh to between her legs and, incredibly, his lips followed. Unerringly, he found her center.

White-hot bolts of heat began to devour her. Reality slipped away, leaving only ecstatic sensations and an unearthly sensuality. An intolerable urgency took her over. If she had ever had any patience, it deserted her. Their time together was ticking away.

"Please, Des. *Now.*"

He straightened over her, and with one strong stroke, he entered her. A pleasure so hot and intense flashed through her that she could only call his name again and again.

As if they had been lovers for years instead of hours, their bodies moved together in an astounding synchronicity. A molten pressure began to build within her. It grew, expanded and stretched until there was nothing left of her but that. She became need.

Hours later, minutes later, seconds later—she couldn't tell—it burst apart inside her with a volcanic force, taking her into another dimension where only love and passion existed. Dimly something occurred to her. They hadn't used protection, not last night, not now. She could be pregnant.

She prayed she was.

Des drew the covers over Kit and pulled her sleeping body closer. Soon it would be a new day and they would once again be occupied with finding out who really killed Cody Inman. But for now he could concentrate on the amazing woman who lay in his arms.

She presented a big problem to him.

He loved helping her, protecting her, and despite the circumstances of the murder, he had loved this time they were having together. Most of all, he loved spending the night together with her. And he loved the many ways he had come to know her.

He loved watching her think, so much so that he often forgot to. He loved the way she came apart in his arms, and the fact that she could make him come apart, too.

In her sleep, she stirred against him, and for no particular reason, he smiled. Silly, he supposed, but there it was. He loved everything about her that he could think of.

Hell, he even loved her independence and stubbornness. But he could feel her constantly trying to put an emotional distance between them. It was obvious she didn't want to be close to him, and that was the problem.

He couldn't think of anything that would make him happier than to be close to her for a long, long time.

He loved her.

He *loved* her.

He went still.

His big problem had just become gigantic. How was he ever going to have her completely? How was he going to keep her by his side day in and day out for the rest of their lives?

He didn't know, but he would definitely have to figure out a way. He had never been in love before, never known this aching need to make a woman part of him and his life. And with Kit, his logical, problem-solving abilities went right out the window.

She stirred against him again. This time, he did what seemed so natural. He shifted over her and pushed into her. And as if she had been made just for him, her velvet sweetness welcomed and tightly sheathed him. At that moment he wasn't entirely sure she *hadn't* been made just for him. They fit together so perfectly, he could stay that way forever.

In the next instant he knew he couldn't. He wanted her too damn much.

He gritted his teeth, trying to hold himself back from his release until she was fully awake and could enjoy their lovemaking as much as he did. But it was hopeless.

Slowly and surely he thrust in and out of her, and little by little she began to respond, lifting her hips to receive him in a perfect harmony that made the blood sing and race in his veins.

Her eyes drifted open, and she smiled up at him. He smiled back. In this one way he could make her his, if only for this small space of time. And he proceeded to do just that.

"What time is it?" Kit asked, snuggling in a contented way against him.

Des automatically reached for his watch on the

nightstand, then realized he had taken it off in his room. "It's morning."

She chuckled, and he softly kissed her. When he pulled back from her, he saw a look of amazement on her face.

"What was that for?"

"It was a reward for laughing. You don't do it enough."

She smiled. "Gee, you're easy. Did Donna know that?"

He grimaced in mock pain. "Will you please get off the subject of Donna? I'm in bed with you, not her."

"It's not good enough. I won't be happy until she *knows* you're in bed with me not her. I want her to be as jealous of me as I was that night of her."

"Even without knowing about us spending our nights together, I imagine she's plenty jealous of you already. As a matter of fact, none of the girls I dated have even come close to accomplishing all that you have."

"You mean running the ranch?"

"The Double B is not just a ranch, Kit. Under your guidance, it's become one of the most successful ranches in the world."

She was silent for several moments, but he could see her thinking and wondered what she was going to say next. Before her, he had never even cared what a woman might say next. But Kit had broken the mold. No other woman would ever again do for him.

"I heard that Donna became a lawyer."

"That's right."

"And you still don't think she has accomplished what I have?"

"Not even close."

"I also heard she married and now has two children. Sorry, but any way you look at it, *that* is a wonderful accomplishment."

"I have to agree with you there."

She looked up at him, a frown on her face, laughter in her eyes. "You should have continued to disagree with me."

"Sorry. Next time I will."

"Really? Okay, I'll test you. Let's see... Back when you and Donna were both sixteen, you didn't really like her all that much, did you?"

Thankful for whatever had put her in a good mood, he threw back his head and laughed. "I was *sixteen,* Kit. My hormones were raging. Of course I liked her."

"You just failed the test miscrably."

"Sorry, but I'll repeat it again. You're in this bed with me and she's not. Plus, I seem to recall that I dated Donna only a few months before someone else came along."

"How few?"

He rubbed his face. "I don't know. That was a long time ago. And besides, I can't think of any reason why I should remember."

"Okay," she said, sounding partly pacified. "So who was the girl who came along after Donna?"

"I'm hungry. Let's get dressed and go find some breakfast."

"You're changing the subject."

"Because I don't like to take on subjects I can see no way of winning." He patted her bottom lip with a finger, emphasizing each word.

She kissed the pad of his finger. "I never would have thought it, but you're a cowardly man, Des Baron."

"What I am is a *smart* man."

She laughed, and he felt his heart swell. Kit looked relaxed and happy. More importantly, she wasn't trying to put emotional distance between them now. He felt as if he had won at least a small victory.

"It was Melissa, wasn't it?"

"What?"

"Your next girlfriend was Melissa, wasn't it?"

He groaned. "You know this isn't fair."

"I think I said something like that not too long ago and it didn't do me a bit of good."

"But you didn't have any boyfriends when you were growing up, which gives you the distinct upper hand in this type of conversation."

She smiled. "I know. Tell me about Melissa."

"No."

"I heard she became a pediatrician."

"You seem to hear a lot."

Her green eyes glittering with mischief, she nonchalantly lifted one bare shoulder. "I manage."

A sudden thought struck him, a *hope.* "So do you want to have children someday?"

Without moving a muscle, she withdrew from him. "Now that you mention it, I'm hungry, too. I'll take a quick shower and then we can go eat." She slid out of his hold and off the bed. Belatedly, she seemed to remember she was naked. Hastily she reached for the bulky bedspread and wrapped it around herself.

"You didn't answer my question."

"You'll get over it."

He came up on one elbow. "I'm sorry I didn't use protection, Kit. I wasn't prepared."

"Don't worry about it. And you didn't answer *my* question, either."

"The one about Melissa? They're not even in the same category."

"They were both questions."

"Do you want to have children, Kit?"

She looked away. "More than anything in the world." Before he could respond, she vanished through the bathroom door. Soon afterwards, he heard her turn on the shower.

Once again she had withdrawn from him, but this time it was okay. He had gotten the answer he wanted. She wanted children. He did, too. Maybe that was the leverage he needed.

Kit sat in the tub and allowed the water from the shower to rain down over her. She didn't know what had gotten into her, teasing Des as she had, but it had been fun, and she had thoroughly enjoyed herself. She was also bone-deep happy that they had made love again.

Besides, Des had seemed to forget that he should

be angry with her. In fact, he might even feel that in some sort of odd way they were even now. After all, his lovemaking had driven her right over the edge of sanity. Some time in the night, she could even remember pleading with him to put her out of her agony of need.

He had. He had driven into her hard and fast, taking her to the precipice of ecstasy and then beyond. And then he had followed her, making it absolutely perfect.

It would be another memory for her when Des decided to go his separate way from her. But ultimately she now knew that her memories would be cold comfort. They could never even come close to the reality of Des and this time they had spent together.

The fact that she would probably see him around the ranch from time to time was going to make it even harder on her. How was she going to remain carefree and casual when her heart and body would be crying out for him?

Lost in thought, she remained where she was for a while, until she realized that she was wasting time thinking about the gloomy future when the present was waiting for her.

But when she hastily toweled off and returned to her room, she found that Des had gone to his. It was just as well, she told herself, and wished for more conviction. Still, they had to find Mike today, and the sooner they could get started the better it would be.

She picked up the phone and called the Double B's business office. Luckily Mike had given his sister's name as next of kin, and her address was on file, too.

Ten

At the restaurant, Kit and Des placed their breakfast order, then she went to call the apartment of Mike's sister to make sure he was there. He was.

"Mike?"

"Yes?" He sounded tired.

"This is Kit Baron. I need to talk with you."

"Ms. Baron?"

"That's right. I'm sorry to bother you at a time like this, but I'm in town and would like to come over and talk with you if I may."

Mike was quiet for several seconds. She could imagine how surprised he was to hear from her.

"What about?"

"I'd rather not say until I get there." Cody's murder was not news to be broken over the telephone.

"I don't understand what this is about."

"We'll tell you all about it when we get there."

"We?"

"Des Baron is with me."

His stunned silence filled her ears. "If you've come all this way to fire me, you could have saved yourself the trouble. I quit."

"I'm sorry to hear that, but listen, please don't worry about your job right now. Now is not the time for you to be making major decisions. And you're not in any trouble with us. I have no intention of firing you."

"Then what is it?"

"There's just something we'd like to discuss with you."

"Okay, then. Uh, do you need directions over here?"

"We'll get a map. Oh, and we'll be there in about an hour, if that's all right."

"I guess. See you then."

Back at the booth, Kit sent a troubled look at Des. "I hope he's going to be able to help us, because if he can't…"

Des reached over and trailed his fingers down her cheek in an extraordinarily tender way. "If he can't help us, we'll find another way. The main thing for now is that we're doing something to help you, rather than sitting around, waiting for that laughingstock of a sheriff to decide to arrest you. So for now, try not to worry."

She *was* worried and fervently hoped Mike would

be able to give them at least one piece of information that would help her. But what was worrying her even more was the challenge she faced of living without Des once he grew tired of her.

Angie Stillwell's apartment was small and consisted of a kitchen that was separated from the tiny living area by a bar. Through a doorway, she could also see a bedroom and bath. Empty cardboard boxes littered the floor. A framed photograph of Mike with his arm around a beautiful teenaged girl held place of honor on a side table. The young girl—Angie, she guessed—was staring adoringly up at him.

"Thank you for seeing us, Mike," Kit said as a way of starting off. "First of all, I want to tell you how sorry we were to hear of your sister's death. You have our deepest sympathy."

"Thank you." His tone was flat, wooden, as if he had spent all his emotions and had none left. Then, as if it were too much effort to continue standing, he dropped down into the chair opposite them.

She glanced at Des. He nodded at her encouragingly. "Mike, I'm afraid I have some more bad news. The morning you left the Double B, Cody Inman was killed."

Mike stared at her blankly; then his face crumbled into utter sadness.

"I'm sorry to have to be the one to break the news to you. Were you close?"

"No."

"Still, I know it's a shock. It has been for all of

us.'' She paused. "Mike, the reason we're here is because we were told you were at the poker game that took place the night before Cody was killed. And we were wondering if anything happened during the game, or if anything was said, that might help us figure out who would want him dead.''

He glanced at the photograph she had noticed before. "I don't know about anyone else, but...I did.''

"Excuse me?'' She exchanged a quick look with Des.

"I wanted him dead, though when I left the ranch that morning, I wasn't sure he was.''

Des's dark brows rose. "I'm afraid I'm not sure what you're saying, Mike.''

Mike exhaled a long weary breath, then gazed down at his palms. The calluses there spoke of hard, physical work. "Right before I left the ranch to come up here to bury my sister, I found Cody in the barn and had a hell'uva argument with him. Then I picked up a shovel and gave him a good whack in the head.''

"But why?'' Kit asked incredulously. She could hardly believe that Mike was actually confessing.

"A while back, Cody came up here with me on a visit. He was kind'a friendly with Angie, but at the time I didn't notice anything unusual. I was just glad they seemed to hit it off. Later I learned that he had come up here several times to see her.'' His voice broke. "It was my fault. I should have paid more attention. Angie was a bit slow, you see. And when any man paid attention to her, she just opened up like a flower. And I *knew* that.'' He rubbed the heels of his hands against his eyes, then slowly shook his head. "I can't believe she kept his visits from me. She always told me everything, but she must have known I would try to stop it."

"Why would you have?"

He met her gaze. "Cody was okay to hang out with now and then, but he wasn't someone you would want your sister seeing on a regular basis."

"So you're saying Cody dated her?"

"I'm saying he got her pregnant, then told her he didn't believe he was the father and she was on her own." A tear trickled down his cheek. "The *bastard*. She was a good girl and believed everyone was good. And when he dumped her like he did…" Another tear spilled unnoticed down his cheek. "I guess by then she was too ashamed to tell me, but a friend of hers who worked with her called me and told me the story."

"When was that?" Des asked.

"The evening of the poker game. So when Cody showed up for the game, I was madder than hell at him. Except I didn't want to say anything to him with all the guys around." He spread out his hands. "I was trying to protect her, just like I'd done all her life." A sob broke from him. He paused to compose himself and wiped his face. "So anyway, I waited until after the game was over with. I confronted him and told him he damn well would make it right by Angie, but the son of a bitch just laughed and went off to drink some more." The tears started again. "I didn't sleep much that night, and by the next morning,

I'd made the decision that I would quit the Double B, move up here and try to help Angie. But the next thing I knew, the police called and told me she had committed suicide.'' More tears flooded down his face.

"So you went looking for Cody?"

"Right." Mike wiped away the tears and gazed at Kit. "I was standing outside the barn when you two had your argument."

She shook her head uncomprehendingly. "But Tio was outside the barn when I went out."

"I was at the back door. I waited until you left, then went in and confronted him. Things got out of hand. First thing I knew, I picked up a shovel and hit him upside the head."

"Was that the fatal blow?" Des asked.

"It was the only blow. He went down, but still it didn't occur to me then that I might have killed him. I don't know why—it just didn't. Maybe I was just too busy thinking about what I had to do when I got up here." He shrugged. "But somewhere in the back of my mind I think I did know it. I just wouldn't let myself think about it too much, you know?"

Kit nodded. "I know."

"That's the whole story."

"One more thing. What did you do with the shovel? It hasn't been found."

"I don't know. I guess I threw it down before I left."

"Where?"

He shrugged again. "I wasn't paying attention."

Des cleared his throat. "Mike, are you willing to tell the sheriff what you just told us?"

Bleakly Mike nodded.

Kit barely resisted the urge to reach out to Mike and comfort him. Oddly enough, she felt nothing but compassion for him. "Will you come back with us now?"

With a visible effort, he roused himself out of the lethargic stupor into which he had fallen. "First I've got to finish packing up Angie's things, though there's not really much. But I can't think what to do with a lot of this stuff. Guess I'll give her clothes away."

"I'll help you," Kit said impulsively. "You pick out the things you'd like to keep, then we'll pack them up and put them in storage. After that I'll arrange for the rest of her things to be given to charity."

"All right." He clasped his hands together between his legs and bowed his head. "Ms. Baron, I'm real sorry for the trouble I've caused you. It wasn't on purpose. None of it was."

"I know that, Mike. I know."

Des.

Where was he tonight?

Kit was curled up in her cashmere robe on the corner of the sofa in her living room. A small lamp shining in a corner provided light, along with the fire that crackled warmly in the nearby fireplace.

She should feel contentment, she reflected sadly. The hunt for the real killer was over. Mike had been arrested and would be charged with manslaughter. Des was pretty sure that with his help, and once Mike's story was heard, he would draw a light sentence. But all she felt was an aching emptiness. She had never really had Des, yet it felt as if she had lost him.

She had fought hard for her independence and had always been proud of it. And even in the middle of those two blazing nights when Des had held her and made love to her, she had never considered giving up her independence.

Yet she had become accustomed to his arms, to his company, to his good-humored moods and his bad. She had become accustomed to *Des*. And now that she thought about it, accustomed was too mild a word. Addicted was more accurate.

"Hi."

She jumped at the soft deep voice and looked around. "Des?"

"Sorry," he said, walking slowly over to her. "I didn't mean to frighten you."

"You didn't. It's just that…my mind was somewhere else. What are you doing here?"

He sat down beside her on the sofa, leaving a cushion between them. "I came to see how you were."

"Oh, I'm fine, just fine. I've already called Tess and Jill. They were thrilled."

"That's good." He tilted his head to one side. "You must be tired. It's been a gruelling few days."

"I guess so."

"You don't sound too sure."

"No, you're right. It has been gruelling."

"You must also be glad it's all over."

She wrapped her arms around herself. "It was like a weight on me to have even one person think I could kill a man."

"Trust me. No one who really knows you could ever think you would be capable of that."

Her lips quirked. "Which of course leaves out the sheriff."

"Definitely. You know, if there's one thing I've learned listening to Mike's story, I suppose it's that you don't know what you're capable of until it comes right down to it, what you'll do in any given situation, especially if your reason is strong enough."

"That's right."

"I don't suppose the sheriff apologized to you?"

She chuckled. "I won't hold my breath."

"I can get him to apologize if you'd like."

She didn't doubt for a minute that he could. "The man is vermin. Not worth another second of my life."

"That's a good attitude to have."

Something in his expression caught her attention. "You plan to do something to him, don't you?"

Des nodded. "Let's just say I'm going to do something *about* him. As it happens, the state's attorney general is a friend of mine, and I'm going to have a talk with him. The only reason I haven't contacted him before now is because I didn't want anyone to be able to say you got out of this mess because of favoritism. But now all bets are off."

"Des, don't go out on a limb because of me."

His eyes softened as they rested on her. "I can't think of a better reason."

"No. I don't want you to risk anything."

"Risk won't even come into it. And there's no limb. You said it yourself. The man is vermin. In addition, he's a rotten sheriff. He didn't look at anyone else besides you as the potential killer. He needs to be relieved of any type of position where he can destroy someone's life because he sees something in it for himself."

"When you put it like that, I can't disagree with you. I wouldn't like to think of any innocent person's life being ruined."

"And what about Ada de la Garza? I thought I'd leave her to you."

She grinned. "I haven't forgotten about her, and, as it happens, I've decided she *is* worth a few more seconds of my life."

"I can't wait to hear *this*. What have you planned and do you need any help?"

She chuckled. "No. I don't need or want any help on this one, thank you. I'm going to call the editor of her paper and make sure the true story of what happened to Cody, Mike and Angie is told...by *another* reporter. That request alone should put the brakes on any advancement she might have been hoping for."

"If you didn't, I was going to."

"There's more. When I tell the editor how she acted, he might just show her the door. In fact, from now on I'm going to keep an eye on her career. I know that type of journalism is what is selling today, but it doesn't belong in any respectable newspaper."

He smiled. "Perfect."

His mouth... Beneath her robe she felt her nipples harden. She remembered every detail of how his mouth had felt on her lips, on her breasts, on her entire body. "So how about you? You must be relieved, as well. Now that you're no longer going to do trial work, you can have that luxury of...time. Isn't that what you said?"

"And I said I was going to be *home*."

"Home." She repeated the word.

"I'm glad you brought that up."

"You've changed your mind?" She didn't want him to, she suddenly realized. She had dithered over which situation would be less painful for her. She still didn't know, but her indecision was over. She wanted him near her.

"No, but I've discovered something very important in the last few days. Or rather, I should have said I've discovered *someone*."

"S-someone? What are you talking about?" An unthinking fear clutched at her.

"You, Kit. I've discovered *you*."

She stared at him, quite sure her mind had played a trick on her. She couldn't have heard right. And if she had, she had to be misinterpreting what she was hearing. "What?"

With extreme tenderness, he took her hand in his. "Marry me, Kit. I know I'm doing this badly, but I've never done it before."

She felt the blood drain from her face. "What are you doing?"

"I'm asking you to marry me."

"No." Her answer was spoken before she had time to think about it, but once it was out, she knew she had given the right one.

Silence ricocheted around the room. It hit the walls with an awful percussion. It was horrible, and she rushed to stop it. "I—I can't marry you, Des. Please understand."

"I'm sorry, but I don't. Frankly, I thought you'd jump at the chance. I remember a time when you were throwing yourself at me."

"I never did that." Now he had her on the defensive, a place where she didn't want to be. How could she have forgotten his stellar reputation as an attorney who could tear the opposition to shreds?

"Yes, you did."

"You're talking about the time when my sisters and I went after you because of our father's will. That's a totally different situation."

"Not really. The will still stands."

"But the circumstances have changed. Tess and Jill are happily married now, and they've learned there are more important things in the world than to have controlling interest in a company."

"I agree they're happy and have learned that, but don't kid yourself. If somehow they were handed control, they would take it so fast your head would spin."

It was true, she thought morosely. But she no

longer cared who got what percentage. He would never believe her, though, nor would he understand.

"*But* if you and I married," he said, persisting, "*you* would have the advantage over your sisters."

"You would still vote your shares."

If there was one thing she now knew Des had in spades, it was integrity. No matter what anyone else said, he would always do what he thought was best. And she was positive he would think keeping control of his fifty percent was best. Besides, what man wouldn't want to have voting control of one of the richest companies in the world?

"My wife's opinion would be very important to me. I would consult her on all decisions."

His wife. She could barely stand to think about it. A surge of jealousy nearly brought her to her knees. The mere idea of another woman lying in his arms at night, eating breakfast with him each morning, made her almost sick. "I'm sure you would," she said in the most noncommittal voice she could manage.

What irony. He was offering her everything she had ever thought she wanted on a silver platter, and she was turning him down because he wasn't offering her his love. She had to be mad.

"The idea of that control doesn't tempt you even a little bit?"

Briefly she thought about lying and saying yes, but that would only give him more fuel for his argument. Plus, she needed to be as truthful as she could. She could get caught up in a web of lies. As long as he didn't ask her point-blank if she loved him, she would be fine. But love was the one word he hadn't used. "No. Not at all."

He raked his hands through his hair. "Then what is it, for Lord's sake?"

"There's no point in talking about this anymore."

"There's every point, because I don't understand. We have so much in common. We both love the ranch and the memories of it. We even both want children."

"Children? *That's* what this is about? You want children, and I happen to be handy, with all the necessary equipment to have them for you?"

Frustration creased his face. "Sure, why not?"

Now it all made sense to her. Des had accomplished a great deal in his life. He had left a positive mark on his chosen profession, and he was financially secure. But most of all, he had reached that age when a man started to think of children to carry on his name, his genes.

"How much of this has to do with the fact that we didn't use protection?"

"I hadn't even thought about it."

"I'm not pregnant, Des. I know it for a fact." She wished with all her heart she could be, but she had started her period a couple of hours ago.

"That's too bad. But after we're married, you could get pregnant. Why not, Kit? Think about it. Wouldn't you love to have a little girl with curly red hair and sparkling green eyes running free over the Double B?"

Truthfully, she wanted a child so badly she could almost taste it, a child she would raise in love rather than fear. A little girl, as he'd said. Or perhaps a little boy with the quick intelligence and dark good looks of his father.

"Think about how happy she would be when we gave her her first pony," he said, his deep voice continuing to hammer away at her. "Think about the wonder she would feel when she saw her first calf being born. Think about a little girl who would love this land as much as you and I do."

She could feel her strength beginning to crumble. "You're talking about a marriage of convenience," she said desperately. "No child should be brought into a loveless marriage."

"Our child would be loved."

"Of course it would. But he or she would know, Des. She would be able to *feel* that something was wrong between us. She might not know what she was feeling at first. But later, when she was older, she would realize that there was no love between us, and believe me, it would make her desperately unhappy."

"Not if we were the best of friends, and, Kit, I do consider you my friend."

She couldn't stand one more second of his badgering. Any second she was going to crack. "Can't you just take *no* for an answer, Des? *Just take no.*"

He looked at her for several moments, his expression shuttered. "When you put it like that, I guess I have to."

Kit couldn't sleep. Des wouldn't stay out of her mind. Every word he had ever said to her came back to her, as did every stroke of his hand on her skin. But most of all, the memory of the way he had made love to her burned in her brain, in her body.

She tossed and turned for hours, reliving every moment of his marriage proposal. Had she done the right thing by turning him down?

If she married him, the pain would be enormous, because she would always know he didn't love her. And she didn't think she was strong enough to live with him day in and day out for the rest of her life knowing that.

Yet there would also be tremendous pain trying to live without him, and her only comfort would be in knowing he wouldn't wake up one day and feel trapped. He would be free in case he ever truly fell in love.

The question was, which pain would be worse?

She paced the night away, and just before dawn, she took Dia out for a ride. He relished the run, his blond mane and tail streaming out behind him, his long legs easily eating up the distance.

The last time she had ridden him, she reflected sadly, she had been another person. In comparison to the way she felt now, she had been immature then. She hadn't truly understood what love was all about. She hadn't even begun to imagine the ecstasies and the heartbreak it could hold. She had considered herself in complete control of her life. She had felt young and strong.

Now she only felt old.

The wind whipped through her hair, and the cold

air bit at her skin. But no matter how far or how fast she rode, she couldn't resolve her question.

There was only one thing she knew. No matter what had happened between them, Des had remained an honorable man. And by turning down his proposal of marriage, she had hurt his male pride. If nothing else, she owed him the truth.

She turned Dia back toward the homestead.

"Kit?"

She glanced over her shoulder, then went back to brushing Dia down, trying to build up her courage to go see Des. "Hi, Tio."

Tio had come to the ranch years before she was born and had made it his home. He was one of those men who seemed ageless, but his dark brown skin was as tough as leather. "How are you this morning?"

"Fine, just fine." He ambled up to her, took off his hat, then put it back on again. "Congratulations on finding out who killed Cody."

"Thanks."

"'Course we all knew you didn't do it."

She threw the brush into a bucket, then patted Dia's neck. "Thanks for your faith in me, Tio. It really means a lot to me."

"Oh, I wasn't the only one. I hope you know that. Most of us knew you were innocent. It was just that…"

Tio obviously wasn't just passing the time of day as she had originally thought. He had something he definitely wanted to say to her. She closed Dia in his stall. "Just what?"

Tio gave a shake of his head. "Just that *damn* sheriff. I have to say, I don't take a quick dislike to many men, but I shore did him."

She smiled. "I know what you mean."

"Uh-huh." He glanced away, then back at her. "So I did something."

"What?"

"Well, you know, I was just outside the barn when you rode out after fightin' with Cody. Then, later, when I went in and I found Cody..." His lips came together, and he gave another shake of his head. "Well, I tell you right now, I was downright shocked just about out of my boots at finding him dead like that."

"I can well imagine," she said with sincere sympathy. At the same time, she was having a hard time figuring out what he was trying to tell her.

"And there that shovel lay, big as you please, with his blood all over it."

"You *saw* the murder weapon?"

"Oh, yeah. It wasn't that far away from him."

"But, Tio, no one has been able to find it."

"Yeah, I know. See, now and again, I'll read a mystery, and I sure do enjoy 'em. So when I saw that shovel, I decided it wouldn't hurt a thing in the world to hide it until I saw which way the wind was gonna blow."

Her mouth dropped open. "You *hid* it?"

He adjusted his hat. "Shore did. See, I remembered

your argument with Cody, and I got to thinkin' how you're always in and out of the barn, doin' stuff, and the like. And, well, I wasn't shore just exactly what had happened, but my thinkin' was that mornin' that it might be best to just hide the damn thing for a while. So I just up and took it out and buried it under some rocks in a ravine. When that sheriff came huffin' and a puffin' around, trying to make you out as guilty, I knew I'd done the right thing." He shrugged. "Then it snowed."

She stared at him, speechless.

"Don't see no point in diggin' it up now," he added.

"Tio, don't you realize that if the sheriff had found it, you could have gotten in big trouble?"

"Never gave it no mind at all."

"I would have been really upset if that had happened."

"Didn't."

Impulsively she went over and hugged him. To her surprise, his face turned beet red. "I can't tell you how much I appreciate your loyalty."

With a great big grin on his face, he stepped back from her and touched the brim of his hat. "Anytime."

Still reeling from the information Tio had given her, Kit rang Des's doorbell. The last time she had visited this house, she reflected, it had been right before the death of Des's father. Thankfully, after her own father had died, she'd had the opportunity to grow close to her Uncle William. He had been so dear to her, so kind. She supposed that if she needed another reason to tell Des the truth, it would be to honor Uncle William. But she didn't need another reason. She only needed courage.

Des opened the door dressed only in a pair of jeans. She had lived all her life on a ranch where jeans were the norm, but Des looked better in jeans than any man she had ever seen. Her courage threatened to desert her.

Des frowned down at her. "Is something wrong?"

"No. May I come in?"

"Why?"

"I have a couple of things to tell you, one of them being about an amazing encounter I just had with Tio."

"And I would be interested in this because...?"

He definitely wasn't making this easy. "Because it concerns the murder."

He immediately stepped out of the way and gestured toward a door midway down the hall. "Go into the office."

She repressed a sigh. Obviously he wanted to keep things strictly business between them.

As soon as she walked into the office, she was immediately enveloped by a warm familiarity. Uncle William's big desk still sat in the same place as it had when he was alive. Large picture windows overlooked the snow-covered landscape and allowed in a flood of morning sunlight. A worn leather chair beckoned by a blazing fire. A nearby table held a rack of pipes and a humidor. Everything about the room soothed her.

"I see you haven't changed anything."

"I haven't seen any need to."

"I wouldn't, either."

"You mentioned Tio?"

He wanted her to get right to the point. This time she couldn't repress her sigh. "Yes. When I got back from my ride, Tio sought me out and told me that he hid the shovel Mike hit Cody with."

"You're kidding."

"No."

"Did he say why?"

"Out of loyalty to me."

He rubbed the side of his clean-shaven face. "I didn't even think of that possibility, but now that I do, it makes perfect sense."

"Tio also said he didn't think much of the sheriff."

"He's got good taste."

She smiled. "He's a good man."

"So where's the shovel?"

"In some ravine somewhere. I doubt we'll ever find it, and I don't see any reason to even go looking for it."

"I don't either." His gaze turned brooding. "So you have something else to tell me?"

She nodded. It was now or never. "It's about you asking me to marry you last night."

"You've said everything you need to."

"I didn't tell you the entire reason I turned you down."

He folded his arms across his bare chest. "You don't need to. You said no. That's more than enough."

"You don't understand."

"Oh, I understand *no* perfectly. Granted, I did try to change your mind at first, but you finally convinced me. I don't need further convincing."

"Okay, let me put it this way—I didn't tell you the entire *truth*, and I think you deserve it."

"If there's one thing I've learned by practicing law, it's that what a person deserves and what a person gets are two entirely different things."

One way or the other, she was determined he was going to listen to her. "Des, I *love* you."

Every muscle in his body stilled. "Would you repeat that?"

"I love you—too much to agree to a loveless marriage. It would end up being a trap for you. One day you'd fall in love with someone and end up resenting me and our marriage and maybe even our children."

He threw back his head and laughed.

Of all the reactions she had expected, that was the last. "Des?" she asked quietly. "Why are you laughing?"

"Honey, everyone should have the problems you and I have."

"I don't understand."

"You're smart. Figure it out."

She had never felt more stupid in her life. "Tell me."

"I love you, Kit. I love you irrevocably, completely and madly."

It couldn't be possible. Tears sprang into her eyes and hope trickled into her heart, but she had taught herself to be cautious. "Are you sure?"

"Did I leave out positively?" He drew her to him and spoke huskily. "I love you, Kit Baron. Our marriage won't change your last name, but it will change the rest of our lives for the better. Will you marry me?"

She began to laugh with pure happiness and threw her arms around him. "I may be slow, but I'm not a complete idiot. Of *course* I'll marry you."

He kissed her, and she returned the kiss with all her heart and soul.

Epilogue

Spring arrived at the Double B with a profusion of color. A gentle breeze rippled through colorful stands of Indian Blanket and Paintbrush. Newly planted tulips and daffodils held their pretty heads high. A just-built gazebo decorated with garlands of wild daisies stood in a freshly mowed meadow not far from the homestead.

As if she were also planted, Kit stood rooted before the cheval mirror in a corner of her bedroom. She had worn her hair down as Des had requested, but unsatisfied with what she saw, she flicked at the red curls, tugged at the ivory satin skirt of her tea-length wedding gown and readjusted the garland of spring flowers on her head.

Tess glided up behind her. "Stop fussing, Kit. I've never seen you look more beautiful."

"Or radiant," Jill added, coming up on her other side.

Kit smiled at the image of her two pregnant sisters in the mirror. Tess had just discovered she was pregnant and Jill was due in a month.

She couldn't wait to be an aunt, or for that matter a mother. She and Des planned to start on that project tonight. For their honeymoon, they were going to the island of *Serenity,* which Des owned with Jill's husband, Colin Wynne, and she couldn't wait.

"Considering that 'beautiful and radiant' is the way I would describe you two, I consider those great compliments."

Tess laughed. "The only way you can describe me these days is green with morning sickness."

"Green looks good on you." Kit held out her hand, palm down. "Look at this—I'm actually trembling."

"You've got nothing to be nervous about," Jill said. "Des is madly in love with you."

Tess smoothed her hand over her blond French twist. "He's also one of the world's truly great guys."

"I know. I know. It's just that I never thought I'd ever marry."

Tess grinned. "The only important thing now is that you had the good sense to say *yes.*"

Jill turned Kit around to face the two of them. "We brought you something."

"Oh, you shouldn't have done that. I'm just glad you're here."

"No more than we are." Tess left the room, then quickly reappeared carrying a long box that contained a gorgeous profusion of purple irises that had been tied with an ivory satin ribbon. "Jill and I would truly love it if you would carry these today as your bouquet."

A smile glinted in Jill's bourbon-colored eyes. "Half of them are from my garden, and half of them are from Tess's."

Kit gasped with surprise. "This is so *sweet* of you."

"It's from our hearts," Tess said. "Nick's grandmother gave me my start from her garden. When Jill married, I gave her a start from mine."

"And I've enjoyed them more than I ever thought possible," Jill said. "And, amazingly enough to me, they've actually thrived and multiplied."

"Now we want to give *you* a start, and we thought it would be nice if half came from each of our gardens."

"I'm very touched. Thank you."

A knock on the bedroom door sounded. "Kit?" Des called. "May I come in?"

"*No,*" all three sisters answered in unison.

Jill walked over to the door and spoke through the wood. "What's wrong with you, Des? You know perfectly well that the groom is not supposed to see the bride until the wedding begins. It's bad luck."

"I don't believe in superstitions," he answered. "Besides, Kit and I are going to make our own luck."

Kit placed the bouquet on her bed. Just the sound of his voice had her pulse racing. She was still having a hard time believing that she was actually about to become his wife. But it was true. When she had agreed to marry him, she had entrusted her heart to him, and now she had complete faith that he would always treat it gently.

Jill glanced over her shoulder at Tess. "It's up to you."

She laughed, because she couldn't believe they were actually standing there, debating whether she was going to see Des now or see him in fifteen minutes. Besides, truthfully, she couldn't deny him anything. "I think he's right about our luck."

"Maybe he's got a point," Tess admitted to her. "I mean, after all, how many people are lucky enough to find their true soul mates the first time around? And not only have you and Des managed to do it, but Jill and Colin have done it, and so have Nick and I. All of us are incredibly lucky."

Kit gestured at the door. "So open the door."

Des walked in, and she felt her heart melt. He was wearing a hand-tailored black suit with a blazingly white shirt. She didn't think she had ever seen him look sexier or more handsome, nor had she ever been more in love with him than she was at that moment.

He immediately crossed to her. "You look beautiful, Kit."

Tears of pure happiness misted her eyes. "So do you."

He laughed, and the sound created a flood of joy in her.

Tess planted her hands on her hips and eyed him sternly. "Okay, Des, now you've seen her. So *go*. You'll see her again at the gazebo."

With obvious reluctance, Des stepped away from Kit. "Actually, as much as I wanted to see my bride-to-be, that's not the only reason I'm here. I want to conduct a short business meeting before the wedding begins, and I promise it won't take long at all."

"What?" Tess exclaimed. "Are you out of that amazing mind of yours? Get a grip. This is your *wedding* day."

"She's right," Jill said firmly. "We're *not* having a business meeting today, nor are we having one until you two get back from your honeymoon."

Kit put her hand on his arm. "Is this really that important, Des?"

He smiled down at her. "Besides asking you to marry me, I consider this one of the most important things I've ever done."

Jill's dark brows lifted. "Good grief, what is it?"

He reached into his jacket and retrieved three folded legal documents from its inner pocket. "I have a wedding gift I'd like to present to each of you."

"The *three* of us?" Tess asked. "I don't know what etiquette book you read, but it sounds interesting."

"My own." He patted the documents against his

palm. "I've divided up my fifty percent of Baron International into thirds, one for each of you."

Kit glanced at her two sisters and saw that they were as speechless as she was.

"I won't bore you with the details right now. Just know that as of noon yesterday, when our corporate lawyer officially filed the original documents, you each have full and equal rights in the company, with the stipulation that you'll will your portion to your children in equal parts. That same stipulation will apply to them, and so on and so on into perpetuity."

"Des." Tears flooded Kit's eyes. "What a wonderful thing for you to do."

Jill and Tess stared at him, stupefied.

Jill was the first one to find her voice. "I can't believe you've done this."

He handed her a copy, then did the same for Kit and Tess. "Look for yourselves."

None of them could tear their astonished gaze from him.

"But what about you?" Jill asked.

He chuckled. "Don't worry about me. I've managed to make quite a few valuable investments over the years." He grinned at Kit. "Besides, if I ever go broke, I can live off my wife."

Jill shook her head. "That's not what I meant. Uncle William intended for you to have his share of the company or he never would have willed it to you in the first place."

"The most important thing my father ever taught me was to do what was right. He not only would have approved, but if he's looking down on us right now, he's giving a good old Texas yell."

Kit leaned over and lightly kissed his cheek. "Thank you, Des. It's the best gift you could ever have given us."

His dark eyes glinted with love. "You couldn't be more welcome, my darling, and it was my pleasure. See you at the altar?"

"I'll be there."

"You better be," he whispered. Then, louder, "I'll be the one with a bluebonnet in my lapel." He shot a grin at Tess and Jill, then left with a quiet click of the door behind him.

"I didn't think I could be any happier than I was before he came in," Kit said, brushing the tears from her eyes, "but I am."

"Good, because you deserve all the happiness in the world," Tess said. "In fact, we all do."

She took her sisters' hands in hers. "We've done it. We've come through the fire our father created for us and we have survived. More than that, we're actually thriving. We deserve to be extremely proud of ourselves."

Tess sniffed back her own tears. "You're right."

"Yes, you are." Jill blinked the moisture from her own eyes, reached for the bouquet of irises and handed it to Kit. "So let's go. Colin and Nick are waiting for Tess and I, and you've got the most important date of your life at the gazebo."

Letting out a peal of laughter, Kit cradled the flowers in her arms and headed out the door. Her future was waiting, and she didn't want to keep it waiting one more second.

Des.

* * * * *

Silhouette®

invites you to enter the
exclusive, masculine world of the...

TEXAS
Cattleman's Club

Lone Star Jewels

**Silhouette Desire's powerful miniseries features five
wealthy Texas bachelors—all members of the state's
most prestigious club—who set out to recover the
town's jewels...and discover their true loves!**

MILLIONAIRE M.D.—January 2001
by Jennifer Greene (SD #1340)

WORLD'S MOST ELIGIBLE TEXAN—February 2001
by Sara Orwig (SD #1346)

LONE STAR KNIGHT—March 2001
by Cindy Gerard (SD #1353)

HER ARDENT SHEIKH—April 2001
by Kristi Gold (SD #1358)

TYCOON WARRIOR—May 2001
by Sheri WhiteFeather (SD #1364)

Available at your favorite retail outlet.

Silhouette®
Where love comes alive™

In March 2001,

Silhouette® Desire

presents the next book in

DIANA PALMER's

enthralling *Soldiers of Fortune* trilogy:

THE WINTER SOLDIER

Cy Parks had a reputation around Jacobsville for his taciturn and solitary ways. But spirited Lisa Monroe wasn't put off by the mesmerizing mercenary, and drove him to distraction with her sweetly tantalizing kisses. Though he'd never admit it, Cy was getting mighty possessive of the enchanting woman who needed the type of safeguarding only he could provide. But who would protect the beguiling beauty from *him...?*

Soldiers of Fortune...prisoners of love.

Silhouette®

Where love comes alive™

#1 New York Times bestselling author

NORA ROBERTS

brings you more of the loyal and loving, tempestuous and tantalizing Stanislaski family.

Coming in February 2001

The Stanislaski Sisters

Natasha and Rachel

Though raised in the Old World traditions of their family, fiery Natasha Stanislaski and cool, classy Rachel Stanislaski are ready for a *new* world of love....

And also available in February 2001 from Silhouette Special Edition, the newest book in the heartwarming Stanislaski saga

CONSIDERING KATE

Natasha and Spencer Kimball's daughter Kate turns her back on old dreams and returns to her hometown, where she finds the *man* of her dreams.

Available at your favorite retail outlet.

Where love comes alive™

January 2001
TALL, DARK & WESTERN
#1339 by Anne Marie Winston

February 2001
THE WAY TO A RANCHER'S HEART
#1345 by Peggy Moreland

March 2001
MILLIONAIRE HUSBAND
#1352 by Leanne Banks
Million-Dollar Men

April 2001
GABRIEL'S GIFT
#1357 by Cait London
Freedom Valley

May 2001
**THE TEMPTATION OF
RORY MONAHAN**
#1363 by Elizabeth Bevarly

June 2001
A LADY FOR LINCOLN CADE
#1369 by BJ James
Men of Belle Terre

MAN OF THE MONTH

For twenty years Silhouette has been giving
you the ultimate in romantic reads. Come join
the celebration as some of your favorite authors
help celebrate our anniversary with the most
sensual, emotional love stories ever!

Available at your favorite retail outlet.

Silhouette®

Where love comes alive™